C000001411

WHO WANTS TO DATE A BILLIONAIRE?

LAURA BURTON

BURTON & BURCHELL LTD

FROM THE "WHO WANTS TO...A
BILLIONAIRE?" SERIES.

Who Wants to Date A Billionaire?
By Laura Burton

All characters, themes and storylines are fictitious and any similarities to actual events are purely coincidental. Copyright 2019 Laura Burton. The author holds all the rights. This book is for personal use only, copying any part of this book and distributing it online is strictly prohibited.

First Edition

This book was written in English US. To discuss translation rights, please contact the owner, Laura Burton at laburton08@yahoo.co.uk.

All Rights Reserved. 2019

Edited By R J Creamer

❀ Created with Vellum

CHAPTER ONE

A MATCHMAKER'S DILEMMA

"It's a beautiful day to fall in love!" Emily clasped her hands together and beamed as she looked out of the squeaky-clean window of her top floor office.

"You say that every day," Jacqueline muttered under her breath, but not too quietly that Emily didn't hear it. She furrowed her brows and turned back to look at her young assistant.

"That's because…," she began as she marched across the office and straightened a picture frame on the wall, "…every day is a perfect day to fall in love."

Jaqueline's freckled cheeks grew crimson as she

clutched a white folder to her chest and smiled. "Yes, Ms. Stewart." She bowed her head and bobbed.

Emily tilted her head to the side and studied Jaqueline for a moment. She had narrow arms and a slight frame that any New Yorker woman would be jealous of. She was fresh-faced, with plump lips, and a spray of auburn hair fanned out passed her shoulders. Her fashion sense needed some work: Whoever told her it was okay to wear Crocs to the office? Or at all, for that matter? With a plain brown skirt, no less! She looked like the before picture in Estelle's glamour makeover spread, which reminded Emily she needed to pick up a copy at the subway. The spring edition just released a couple of days ago, and it was vital to keep up-to-date with the latest trends for work.

"What do we have on today's agenda?" Emily touched up her nude lipstick, as she gave herself the once-over at the floor length mirror, then flicked her sleek brown hair back from her shoulders.

"You have a nine o' clock with Mr. Hughes…."

"Ah, Eddie." Emily smiled to herself, then waved her hand at Jaqueline to continue. "Mr. Michaels is coming in at ten-thirty. You have a conference call set up with the investors at one and—"

"Oh right, that's today." Emily tucked in her white satin blouse to her leopard-print pencil skirt and paced the room.

"Cancel all my afternoon appointments. I need to make sure that call goes well."

"I'm sure——" Jaqueline started but stopped short as Emily shot her a look.

"Yes, Ms. Stewart." She bobbed her head again.

Emily resisted the urge to roll her eyes. *You don't have to curtsey to me*, she thought as she looked at her expectantly. On cue, Jaqueline passed over the white folder. Emily flipped it open and lazily thumbed through the pages. After a few moments she looked up at Jaqueline.

"Is there something else?"

Jaqueline's dark eyes widened, and she jumped as if she'd been struck with a bolt of lightning.

"There is one more thing…." Her voice faltered, and she wrung her hands.

"Well? What is it?"

Why is she so timid? Am I scary to her?

Jaqueline's eyes darted around the room unable to make contact with hers.

"My brother is getting married in four months, and I was wondering…."

"Oh, Jaqueline. I thought you'd never ask. I'm so happy you've come to me and, yes, I will help you." Emily picked up her purse and rooted through her Gucci wallet.

"What?" Jaqueline stood, blinking as Emily handed her a business card.

"Ask for Candice, she does the best wax. Ask for HD brows and do not use those nasty tanning beds at the mall. Ask for Joy, she'll do a light natural spray tan." Emily circled Jaqueline looking her up and down.

"It's unfortunate you didn't give me more notice; my hair stylist has a six-month waiting list. Perhaps he has an apprentice who could take a look at you."

Jaqueline opened and closed her mouth like a fish out of water.

"I didn't mean—"

Emily placed her hands on her hips.

"You don't want a makeover and shopping spree? Surely, you're not getting ready for a wedding without any help?" A hint of a frown appeared on Jaqueline's face as she stood up a little more upright.

"I am going shopping with my sister next weekend, and my mom is going to do my hair."

Emily forced a smile. *Such a wasted opportunity.*

"I was hoping that you could—"

Emily clapped her hands, struck by a sudden epiphany.

"Oh, you need to find a date. Well, I'm not sure it's something I could do for free, I mean, you're not a bad-looking girl, but it would take considerable effort on my part to find someone."

"I have a boyfriend," Jaqueline said quickly.

Emily stared at her defiant face and pursed her lips.

"My brother is having a small wedding in Hawaii."

"How romantic." Emily sighed, her eyes glazed over as she imagined standing on the sandy shores surrounded by friends and family with a string quartet playing "Canon in D" as she looked adoringly at the faceless groom in front of her.

"I need to take a couple of days off." Jaqueline's voice was stronger now, she seemed to have found her courage. Emily threw her hands in the air and rolled her eyes.

"Why didn't you just say that at the beginning?"

"You didn't let me finish."

"Yes, sorry, I did get carried away, didn't I? Well make sure you send me the dates you need off, and I'll hire a temp to cover you."

"Thank you, Ms. Stewart." Jaqueline turned to leave.

"You know, if you change your mind about the makeover, the offer is still open."

Jaqueline's smile did not reach her eyes.

"I'll think about it, thank you." She vacated the room and closed the door behind her. Emily shimmied along the white desk and looked out of the window at the skyscrapers across the street. Her office was well-placed in downtown New York. Just a hop, skip, and jump away from Tiffany's – the local hot spot for engagement rings—and a breath away from the

Empire State Building—a popular place for proposals. The yellow phone sitting in its cradle sang loudly in the room, diverting Emily's attention away from the window. Usually phone calls were directed to Jaqueline unless the person had her direct number. With a frown, she lifted the handset and placed it to her ear.

"Find My Companion matchmaking services, Emily Stewart speaking."

"Good morning Emily, this is Matthew Haines."

"Matthew. Right... hello." Emily flipped open her pink diary and chewed the inside of her cheek as she found his name. "Matthew Haines, Investor" was underlined several times. Matthew approached Emily at a business networking event the previous week. She was on the hunt for someone to invest in her business plans and he was the only person who showed any interest.

"A couple of things have come up and the investors have asked me to go ahead with our call alone. I'll provide feedback to them afterward."

"Right...."

"I need to move our call to this morning."

Emily lowered into her large leather chair and crossed her feet.

"Oh, of course, I could move some things around." She placed the phone on speaker and pressed the buzzer next to her phone. Jaqueline opened the door and Emily motioned for her to remain silent and listen.

"What time are you thinking?" Emily attempted to sound bright and breezy, like this was not the most annoying change of events ever. She scrawled a note on her new pink diary and held it up to Jaqueline.

"I wondered if this might be a convenient time?" Matthew's drawl had Emily imagining a retired cowboy sitting in a Texan smokehouse, ready to pony up to some beef brisket while catching the game on the big screen. He sounded far too relaxed to be discussing something as important as this. Emily nodded along.

"Absolutely, that will be fine. I'll just need to put you on hold for a moment while I talk to my assistant."

"Fine by me."

Emily looked up at Jaqueline in horror.

"I need you to cancel my nine o' clock, and tell Mr. Michaels I'll call him later. Reschedule for this afternoon," she murmured to her. Jaqueline nodded quickly and left the room. After taking a deep breath, Emily straightened her back and cracked her knuckles.

"I can do this," she whispered. "Hello again, Matthew, thanks for holding." She fiddled with the Cross pen in her hands as she spoke.

"You have a cute accent there, don't tell me you're a New Yorker?" Emily rolled her eyes and inwardly sighed at the question. *Really? After all these years, I still have an accent?*

"Well, I've been living in New York for almost a decade now," she began.

"So, where are you from? Tell me about yourself."

"Really? Okay." Emily rubbed her palms together and cracked her neck. This conversation was not going the way she had planned.

"I grew up in London."

"London, that's the accent!" Matthew's voice boomed out of the speaker.

"...where I attended Oxford and received straight As." Emily continued, undeterred. "In addition to my studies, I took on extracurricular activities such as charity fundraising, and I earned a black belt in martial arts." Emily inhaled and held her breath. The heavy silence from the other side of the phone prompted her to continue. She exhaled. "I graduated from Oxford university with honors in psychology, focusing on family and relationships. I also studied business, so when I left university, I decided to combine my skills and knowledge and start up a match-making business here in New York."

"If I wanted to know about your education and career, I would have read your resume." Matthew's tone of voice sat like an anvil on Emily's chest.

"Note taken, then what is it you want to know about me?"

"Tell me about your hobbies, your family... what makes you, Emily Stewart?"

Emily looked up at the white ceiling and opened her mouth in surprise. Now that's a question. *What makes me... me?* Emily chewed her lip anxiously.

"I am a people person; it's why I love what I do. I am too busy for hobbies. My work is my hobby. When I'm not meeting with clients and potential matches, I am writing up documentation, studying the market, and networking with other business owners."

"Are you married?"

"No, I'm—"

"So, you're in a long-term relationship, I gather?"

Emily's brows furrowed as she pouted at the hand receiver.

"No, no, I'm far too busy to maintain a relationship of my own." She laughed in an attempt to sound light-hearted. Matthew mumbled something incoherent.

"As you have seen in my proposal, Find My Companion has been in business for almost ten years. We have twelve employees and an extensive client list. I am confident that opening a site in LA is the best move to expand and dramatically grow our business. I assure you; this business opportunity is quite lucrative; market research has shown—"

"I'm just curious…." Matthew's firm voice stopped Emily in her tracks, and she fell silent.

"Yes?"

"What do you know about love?" Matthew's words hit Emily squarely between the eyes.

"I'm sorry," she spluttered, now digging her claw-like false nails into the edge of her desk.

"You're not married… you're not in a relationship. It doesn't sound like a good image for someone who sells love."

"I would have you know that I have a vast number of happy clients who have found—"

"I'm going to make this simple," Matthew said frankly. "Get yourself a husband, then we'll talk about investing."

Emily bit her lip firmly.

"You're not going to invest because I'm not married?" Emily asked incredulously, she surveyed the bare ring finger on her left hand as she spoke.

"If you want to increase your brand and maximize exposure, you need to look the part."

"So, I need to be married?" *I can't believe this!* Emily fumed.

"Ideally, yes."

"Right, so I just go out and get myself a husband and we'll talk again?" Emily glared into the phone.

"Hey, finding a match is what you do, isn't it?" Matthew chortled.

Emily forced a smile as she spun around in her chair and stared out at the sky rise across the road. The large office windows reflected the sunshine, shielding the image of the thousands of faceless workers going about their day.

"Right, piece of cake," she mumbled after she and Mathew exchanged their goodbyes and she hung up the phone.

"Jaqueline!" The cream door swung open and Jaqueline's narrow frame appeared in the doorway.

"Yes, Ms. Stewart?" she asked quickly.

"Bring me the file of our eligible bachelors, and I need you to get me a cinnamon bun from that donut place across the street."

"Actually, Ms. Stewart, someone is sitting in the waiting room for you," Jaqueline said furtively.

"What? Who is it? I told you to cancel my appointments."

"Yes, Ms. Stewart, but this man very much wants to speak with you. He says it's urgent."

Emily stared at Jaqueline's hazel eyes and took a moment to process the news.

"Okay, fine. Send him in." She sighed as Jaqueline nodded and left the room again.

Emily stood up and straightened her pencil skirt

and stared at the door as she prepared for the unexpected visitor to walk through. Soon enough, the door opened again and in walked the tallest man Emily had ever seen. He ducked gracefully as he walked across the threshold and as he stood up straight again, his dark wavy hair flicked back as if in slow motion. Emily stared at him with wide eyes, dazzled by his charming smile while their eyes locked. It took a few moments for her to realize that his mouth was opening and closing when her ears finally decided to tune in.

"… I do appreciate you allowing me to impose on your schedule at such short notice." His voice was low and silky. He had an English school-boy accent. Emily's breath caught in her chest and she grinned widely as she stared at him with sheer delight. His broad shoulders bulged from beneath his designer grey suit and a flash of light by his wrist caught her attention. *Is that a Rolex?*

"I hope you don't mind, this is Robert and Joffrey." He motioned behind him. Emily leaned to the side and caught sight of two huge men standing by the door. One of them was balding at the sides, the other had a full red beard.

"Hello, I'm so sorry I didn't catch your name." Emily stretched out her hand and offered it to the gentleman. He took hers in a firm hold, and she looked down to see the watch on his wrist. *Definitely a Rolex.*

"David," he said softly. They broke contact and Emily gestured to the two white couches sitting across a coffee table in the center of her office.

"Come and take a seat, David." They sat across from each other, while the two men stood motionless by the door.

"I'm a friend of one of your former clients…," David began, offering her a bashful smile. That was normal, most of Emily's clients were nervous during their consultation visit.

"Oh! That's lovely, who?"

"Harold. He said you would be able to help me with my situation."

"If it's love you're looking for, you've come to the right place," Emily said cheerfully.

David smiled broadly at her and then his smile faded as he eyed her seriously. "I require this to be dealt with… sensitively," he murmured.

"Yes, yes, of course. We deal with many clients who need to avoid the public eye. So tell me, David… what line of business are you in? Modeling?' Emily flashed him a cheeky smile. David inclined his head and grinned shyly. His grey eyes twinkled in the sunshine.

"Hospitality," he said humbly. Emily picked up a notepad and pen and crossed her knees.

"I'll just take a few details, if that's all right."

"May I ask a quick question?" David looked up at

her, keeping his head stooped low. He rested his right hand on his knee as he rounded his shoulders.

"Oh, okay...." Emily fumbled with the pages of her notebook in search of a blank page and nervously clicked the pen in her left hand.

"Are you from England, per chance?"

Emily smiled. "Yes, I am."

David sat back and clapped his hands together triumphantly, as though he'd just solved all the world's problems. *Honestly*, she thought to herself, with his posh accent, she'd have thought he went to the London School of Business. "I thought so."

"And you?" Emily asked.

"London," he replied with his hand raised, as if it were a confession.

She had to hold back rolling her eyes. "Where did you go to school?"

"Eton."

Of course.

Emily stared at David as he dragged a hand through his luscious mop of hair. The strands caught the sunlight as it moved, keeping Emily in a trance.

"And you?" David asked with his thick brows raised.

Emily snapped out of her reverie and flicked back her silky hair and sat up straight. "Oxford," she said as she brushed her hand aside. She loosened her grip and her pen dropped to the floor. David smiled at her serenely; apparently, he didn't notice.

The room fell silent as they eyed one another.

"Well, here we are, two foreigners in the Big Apple." Emily said, as she craned her neck and looked out at the large window behind her desk. A window cleaner was on a trolley cleaning the glass. "Although, this feels more like home than England ever was," she mused. She shot back to look at David who sat with his hands together on the couch across from her.

"I beg your pardon, how rude of me. Can I get you a drink?' she blurted out as she motioned to call for Jaqueline.

"No, no I'm fine, thank you." David raised his hands briefly. Emily smiled and settled back into the couch.

"Right, well, what can I do for you, David?"

"I have a predicament."

"Uh huh." Emily bent over and pretended to scratch her ankle as she picked up the pen that was lying on the floor beside her feet. "Care to tell?"

David rubbed his stubbled chin and thought for a moment.

"Off the record?"

"Mr.—"

"Marks." Emily's eyes widened. "As in, the hotel chain?"

"Yes," David said sheepishly.

"Hospitality, eh." Emily laughed to herself and crossed her arms as she eyed the two men standing by the door. *Must be his bodyguards.*

"Mr. Marks—"

"Please call me David."

Rich and charming, very nice.

"Okay, David. Anything said between us is strictly confidential. I assure you, this is not the first meeting I've had with a—"

"Desperate man?"

"I was going to say, client who wants to avoid the press. So, what's the story? Fed up with gold-digging women following you around? Had enough of the rich, beautiful heiresses falling at your feet? Want to find a nice young American girl to fall in love with?"

"Well, simply put, I need to find a wife in thirty days."

Emily looked up from her notepad and stared at David, looking for any sign of sarcasm and found none.

I'll marry you! she thought wildly.

"You...."

"... need to find a wife in thirty days, yes. Do you think you can help me?" he finished for her.

Oh, this is too perfect.

Emily's plump lips curved into an evil smile. "I'm quite confident that can be arranged.

"Ordinarily, I would ask my clients to take a profile quiz on my app." Emily held up her electronic tablet for David to see. "However, due to the time-sensitive nature of your needs, I think it would be more appropriate to get to know you personally instead." Emily buzzed for Jaqueline, who entered the room promptly and eyed the two bodyguards warily as she approached.

"Jaqueline, would you pass my clients to Julian for the rest of the month. This case requires my full attention." Jaqueline nodded and left the room again, quiet as a mouse. "David, I will need a list of available times from you for me to arrange your dates."

"I can do that."

Emily rubbed her palms together and got to her feet. David followed suit.

"Tell me, David, what's your type?"

"I'm sorry?"

"Your type, you know, what sort of woman do you normally go for?"

David frowned. "I don't know," he said slowly. Emily raised her brows in surprise. This was usually the easy part, the part where the client spiels off a list of ridiculously particular characteristics they look for in a potential mate. Short hair, long hair, big hands, small feet, quiet laugh, long legs… the list was endless. And yet, here was a billionaire bachelor who looked like he just strolled off a Hollywood movie set and was capable of getting just about any woman he wanted, yet had no idea what he looked for in a partner? *Fascinating*, Emily thought as she stared at him.

"Okay, let's start off easy. Do you find blondes the most attractive?" she asked pointedly, her pen primed at the notepad, ready for action.

"Well, uh—"

"What interests do you have?"

"Like, hobbies? I travel a lot, I suppose… for work."

"Do you like traveling?"

"Sure." *He probably has his own private jet, of course he likes traveling.* Emily scrawled down some information into her notebook.

"Anything else? Anything you look for at all in a woman?"

"She needs to know her own mind, and can hold up her end of an argument."

"Ah, so you like to be challenged, interesting." Emily wrote into her notebook, encouraged by his participation.

"What about career?"

"What about it?"

"Is it important that she is career driven? Or do

you prefer the stay-at-home wife, sort of woman?"

"I don't mind... she needs to be passionate about something, I guess."

"Body type? Height? Eye color? Any preference at all?" David's face grew crimson at the question. *Is he blushing? This is too adorable.* Half of the women in New York would eat him up! Emily surveyed his expression and leaned forward.

"Can I ask a personal question?" she murmured. David glanced back at the two bodyguards and nodded to them. Slowly they vacated the room, leaving the two of them alone for the first time.

"Have you ever had a girlfriend?" Emily asked seriously. David blinked at her for a moment.

"Would it make me sound like a loser, if I said no?"

"Never?" Emily whistled. "And you want a wife? In thirty days... can I ask why?"

"Look, it's not easy to get dates when you're in my position." David folded his arms.

"Oh, I understand. It's painfully hard to find anyone who would be willing to date a drop-dead-gorgeous businessman who has his own bodyguards."

David laughed. Emily smiled back at him.

"Yes, well that's why I need you."

"I'm more than happy to help, but what's with the time limit? You're not dying, are you?"

"Wow, you really like to pry."

"It's my job to know these things," Emily said simply. David sighed heavily and sat back down on the couch while Emily rested her hands on her hips and leaned against her desk.

"My grandmother is dying."

Emily's hands fell to her sides and she frowned at him.

"Ah, I'm sorry."

"She holds the majority of the shares in the Marks business, and she won't pass them onto me until she's met my wife."

"But you don't have a wife," Emily said quickly.

David grimaced.

"I told my grandmother I eloped a couple of years ago, when she was asking questions."

"Why? And anyway, that sort of information about someone like you, doesn't just stay quiet. It would be in the news, surely. How did you convince your family you were secretly married?"

David got up and walked across the room to look at the photographs hanging on the wall.

"My grandmother is having a birthday party, all the family are expected to attend." David turned around and looked pointedly at Emily. "Including, my wife," he added.

"Fake matchmaking isn't my forte, you know."

Emily cocked her brow as she strolled across the room to him. David raised his hands.

"I know," he said defensively. "I thought you could help me find... the one."

Emily sucked in her cheeks and looked wildly around the room.

"So, you want a smart, opinionated woman to marry you in the next thirty days... oh *and* you want her to be 'the one'?"

David inclined his head. Emily resisted the urge to roll her eyes and laugh.

"Why don't you just hire a woman to pretend to be your wife?" *Pick me!* she silently added, realizing that this could be the perfect scenario for her investors.

"Like I said, I'm looking for more than just a fake wife," David countered. Emily smiled; she liked the sound of that.

"There we go, so we do have a romantic side." She wrote notes down in her book and looked up at him. "Right, I think I have enough to go on here, are you free tonight?"

"You'll have a date set up that quickly?" David seemed surprised. Emily placed her hands on her hips and puffed out her chest.

"I'm Emily Stewart. I can have three dates lined up for you within forty-eight hours."

"Well, yes, in that case. I'll make arrangements to stay in town." David clapped his hands together.

"Quick question: Are you allergic to sushi?"

"Er, no."

"Okay, good. Your first date will be at a sushi bar, and don't worry. I'll keep it nice and discreet. We'll hire out a room in the back, and I'm sure your two pals behind that door will figure out a way to get you there without being seen." Emily sashayed her hips as she walked around her desk and put her notebook down.

"If you leave your contact details with my assistant in the reception, I'll leave you a message when I have some news. Oh, and I assume Jaqueline has passed my pricing list to you?"

"No, she hasn't."

"I'll have her send that on as well, then." Emily held out her hand for David to shake. He took it and the two of them grinned at each other.

"It was a pleasure to meet you, David. I look forward to finding you the perfect wife."

The metal heels of Emily's Jimmy Choo's clicked along the ground as she strutted through the subway station. Crowds of commuters stood around waiting, and the stench of old cigarette smoke clung to the walls like tar. It nearly shielded the overwhelming smell of body odor; nevertheless, Emily had become immune to the offensive aromas in the subway. Getting around in New York took hours, not minutes—no matter which method of transport Emily chose. But she preferred to walk or take the subway rather than sit in traffic watching the taxi meter ticking. Like clockwork, Emily picked up her copy of the new Estelle fashion magazine and a giant hot pretzel from the stands outside the station. She scanned her MetroCard and walked through the barriers absentmindedly as she took a bite of her pretzel and flipped through the pages of her magazine. She grabbed the last seat on the train and avoided eye contact, happily thumbing through the fashion pages.

A couple of African American teenage boys stood by the doors listening to music as they bobbed their heads and made hand signals to each other. A large balding woman swayed side to side as her eyes rolled back in their sockets and she moaned. Not that Emily noticed, of course.

Emily rented out a small apartment downtown, and even though it was only a few stops away, the commute could easily take an hour during commuter times. After nine years, eight months, and sixteen days of doing the journey, Emily was now accustomed to it. She was no longer surprised by the characters she came across; in fact, everyone around her had become invisible.

Emily's phone vibrated. She dabbed her salty lips with a napkin as she put the last of her pretzel down on her lap and picked up the flashing phone from her Gucci purse.

"I'm on the subway. What is it, Jaqueline?"

"I just wanted to check that you *wanted* to set Mr. Marks up with Mandy Price?"

"Yes, what's the problem?"

"I'm surprised, looking at her profile…"

Emily smiled wickedly to herself. "Oh, you don't think she's passionate and opinionated?"

"Sure, she's very opinionated, but I thought—"

"Do I pay you to think, Jaqueline?" Emily asked bluntly.

"Well, I like to think that—"

"There it is again. I don't need someone to think for me. What I need is someone to run errands, and I also did not ask for you to second-guess my decisions."

"Sorry, Ms. Stewart."

"Do not let it happen again."

"My apologies. I'll make those reservations and send out the details to Mr. Marks now."

"See you in the morning, Jaqueline." Emily sighed. She was tired of having to act like a dragon. Yet, this young Jersey girl so often pushed the line. An assistant should not be second-guessing her boss' decisions. She was a confusing girl to Emily, one moment acting timid and shy, then aloof and snappy with her the next. If this was going to work, she figured that telling Jaqueline about the plan was inevitable. With that thought, she puffed out her chest, picked up her pretzel again and she plotted a most-evil plan.

CHAPTER TWO

A Disastrous Date

David clutched the edge of his seat so tightly, he could feel the veins in his arms bulging. He tried not to look bewildered as he watched the young woman sitting across the table order her food.

"I'll have the salmon, but I don't want it smoked, and do you have those little rice rolls wrapped up in leaves?"

The waiter inclined his head and scrawled notes on the minuscule notebook in the palm of his hand.

"I gather you don't eat sushi very often?' David asked politely. Mandy shook her head and offered a laugh in response. David's brows twitched as he resisted the urge to raise them.

"Oh, and be a doll"—she turned back to the waiter again—"get me a tonic water, but not the sparkling kind, it makes me kind of gassy, and we wouldn't want that on a first date!' She threw her head back and roared with laughter, which got caught somewhere in her throat. She coughed and smiled as the waiter walked away.

"So, tell me about yourself. The agency said you're stinking rich!" She flashed a toothy grin. David tried not to look at the red lipstick staining her front teeth.

"Oh, they said that, did they?" He subconsciously ran a tongue across his own teeth.

"Well, obviously they didn't say that, but I didn't need them to. I already knew." She twirled her thick hair between her fingers and eyed him like he was a plaything.

"Really?" David cleared his throat and tried to smile.

Mandy adjusted her pink scarf, the bangles on her arms jangled, and she fluttered her giant false lashes at him.

"I am very intuitive," she murmured. "I have a super power. Do you want to know what it is?"

David shifted uncomfortably in his chair and looked wildly around the room for an escape. He briefly made eye contact with Joffrey, who stood resolutely by the door. Giving a curt nod, Joffrey responded with a small smile.

"Oh, sure…," David said, wondering how quickly he could get out of this situation. From the moment Mandy walked into the secluded dining room, a flume of sickly-sweet perfume flooded the place. It was as if hands were draped around David's neck, squeezing the air out of his lungs.

Mandy leaned forward, with her ample bosom pressed against the table, and stared wide-eyed at David as if offering confession.

"I can read auras," she breathed. Garlic fumes floated through the air as she spoke, his nostrils flared instinctively.

"I'm sorry, what?"

Mandy sat back in her chair and surveyed David with look of total seriousness. "You are the kind of guy with a big heart, you know, and even though you have bags of money, you're totally down-to-earth," Mandy said with her Bronx accent.

"You can tell that by reading my aura?"

The waiter returned with their drinks and silently placed them on the dinner table. Mandy ignored him and nodded fervently at David with a dramatic smile.

"We have a connection you know. I felt it as soon as

I laid eyes on you." David nonchalantly shifted his gaze to Joffrey, who smirked.

Firing him tonight.

"You did?" he asked faintly as he took a sip of his drink. "Well, I don't really know anything about you, perhaps—"

"I thought you'd never ask about me!' Mandy exclaimed gleefully; her blue eyes flashed as she smiled up at the ceiling. "I'm a Gemini, and I have my own business selling crystals. I offer life coaching too."

"Oh, interesting," David said politely.

Mandy nodded appreciatively at him as if she were accepting an Oscar.

"I couldn't be where I am today without my cat."

"Your… cat?"

Mandy pulled out her phone; the back was bedazzled and twinkled in the candlelight.

"Sparkles, he got me through some very dark times." She thumbed through her pictures before holding it out for David to see. What he saw was the grumpiest-looking cat he had ever laid eyes on.

"Isn't he the best?" Mandy said. David looked to see her eyes tearing up. He wanted to cry as well… for different reasons.

"He really helped me go through a nasty divorce." Mandy sighed as she put her phone away. David swallowed and shifted his weight in the creaky chair.

"You've been married?" he asked, glancing at his watch. It seemed like an eternity had passed since they ordered food, when in fact, it had only been ten minutes. Mandy tilted her head to side and shrugged.

"I've been married a few times. It's hard to find a guy to really commit, you know? And a lot of men find my success intimidating," she simpered, pouting her oversized lips at him.

David held his breath as an awkward silence followed.

"Excuse me, Mr. Marks."

Startled, David looked up at Joffrey.

Mandy twirled her hair as she looked up at him curiously.

"I apologize for the interruption, but I've just received word that they need you to call the office." Joffrey's nostrils flared as he spoke. David knew he was lying, and considered giving him a raise.

"I'm so sorry, Mandy, I'll just be a moment." The chair scraped across the floor as he got to his feet. Mandy shrugged and pulled out her phone again as David followed Joffrey out of the room.

"You took your time," David murmured to him once the door closed behind them.

"Sorry, sir," Joffrey said. David couldn't tell if he truly was sorry, though he thought not as his guard tried suppressing a laugh.

"What do you want to do?" Joffrey asked as he scratched the red bristles of his beard.

"Go in there and apologize for me. Say I had to go, um… you can eat my food and—"

"What? I'm not having dinner with her!" Joffrey whispered frantically; his wide eyes were full of fear.

"I can't leave her on her own! Besides, you love sushi. And hey, maybe you two will find something in common?"

"I'm allergic to cats," Joffrey said frankly.

"Well, luckily I'm not paying you to take her home." David clapped a hand on the shoulder of his suit jacket.

"I'm not—"

"Isn't it your job to protect me from people?"

"But, if I'm in there with her, who's going to—"

David raised his finger and smiled.

"Robert is waiting outside," he whispered triumphantly. He gave him a hard look and bit the inside of his cheek.

"Do this for me, please."

The two men stood in the cramped hall to the sushi restaurant having a silent staring contest. After a few moments, Joffrey blew out his breath and his shoulders slumped in defeat.

"Yes, sir."

"You can call me David, you know."

Joffrey laughed.

"Tell you what, I'll go in with you and say good-bye." David clapped him on the shoulder again and the two men strolled back into the room.

D avid paced the bedroom of his penthouse suite as he replayed the conversation he had with Emily. It had been a long week since their meeting. He had been on several dates since then, each one more disastrous than the other. He couldn't figure it out. Emily was the best matchmaker in the city, or so Harold said. He had to see her again, he'd already wasted time... time he didn't have. In theory, this plan was going to be easy.

But then he met Emily; a confident, gorgeous woman, who was also from England! The way she blushed when she dropped the pen on the floor... and tried to pick it up discretely. Her sleek dark hair reached the small of her back, right where her waist narrowed. How could he tell her that she was exactly the type of person he would want to date? How could he persuade her to be with him within the deadline? David swallowed against the dryness in his mouth and coughed.

Snap out of it.

He hatched a plan and picked up his phone.

"Find My Companion, Jaqueline speaking," a sing-song voice echoed out of the speakers in the room.

"Yes, hello. This is David Marks. I need to speak to Emily Stewart."

"I'm sorry, Mr. Marks. Ms. Stewart left the office an hour ago, can I assist you?"

"You can have her give me a call, it's urgent.'"

"Of course. Ms. Stewart will be in touch as soon as possible." David threw his phone on the king-size bed and cracked his knuckles as he kicked off his designer shoes. What was he planning to say?

"Hi Emily, so these women you've set me up with are crazy. Are you single?" He shook his head and laughed at the ludicrous thought. Before he could gather his thoughts, the phone vibrated on his bed.

"Aren't you supposed to be on a date right now?" Emily's musical voice flooded the room after David answered the call.

"About that," he said frankly. Already, his irritation was fading just hearing Emily speak.

"Oh dear, don't tell me you've left poor Mandy all alone, have you?"

"I didn't. Joffrey is having dinner with her," David admitted, sheepishly.

"Your bodyguard is on a date with Mandy? That sounds like a great movie premise." She laughed. The sound was so much more charming than David expected it to be.

"Don't worry, I've got you covered. Your dates have to sign a non-disclosure agreement before they find out who they are meeting. Your secret will be safe."

"Honest question, do you think Mandy is the type of woman who would care about legalities?"

"I think she is the type of woman who has a lot of experience in the courtroom." Behind Emily's professionalism, David sensed a hint of amusement.

"So, you knew she was married?"

"Yes, is that a problem?"

"Three times. That's a red flag, yes." David sighed and rubbed the back of his neck with frustration.

"Why? I'm sure she would be open to signing a prenup."

"I'm not looking to have just any wife! I'm concerned you're not really—"

"Not what?"

David swallowed at the strength in her voice, then paced the room again. A rustling sound interrupted his thoughts and the doorbell rang; the sound ricocheted off the walls of his penthouse.

"Hold on, please," he said as he put Emily on hold. He marched across the suite and opened the door.

"Evening, Mr. Marks. I made sure the chef cooked the steak rare for you."

David smiled and nodded as the portly man walked through the doorway pushing a trolley laden with food.

"Thank you, Joseph."

"Is there anything else I can get for you, Mr. Marks?"

"No, Joseph, thank you."

"Give me a call, anytime."

The door closed behind him. David lifted up the domed silver cloche covering his dinner. The mouth-watering aroma of meat juices flooded his senses. His stomach rumbled in response.

"Are you hungry?" David asked after he took Emily off hold.

"Hungry? That's the last thing I thought you would say to me."

"Well, I'm looking at a steak dinner that's big enough for two here, and I hate to eat alone."

"Are you asking me to come over?"

"Well, it looks like I need to be clearer about what it is I want in a woman." David couldn't stop himself from smiling.

"Oh, I see. This is a business meeting."

He sensed she was warming to the idea.

"With chocolate fudge cake, indeed." David instinctively licked his lips as he anticipated Emily's reply.

"As it is, I haven't had dinner yet. Send across your address and—"

"If you give me yours, I'll have a car come and get you," David offered. Henry, his driver knew the best routes to get across town in optimal time. There was also something about Emily being in his car that excited him.

"They're not going to blindfold me and make me swear not to tell anyone where you live, are they?"

"Who is 'they'?" David laughed as he poured a drink.

"I don't know… you know what I mean." Emily laughed too.

That laugh again! What a wonderful sound.

"All right, sending the address now. I hope that steak is well-done. I hate the sight of blood."

David hung up the phone grinning to himself and looked down at his watch. The night was still young and dangerous ideas were starting to brew.

CHAPTER THREE

A Change of Plan

E mily stared at the stack of bank statements lying on the kitchen table to her small apartment. Living in New York was exorbitant and truth be told, it would make financial sense to live in New Jersey. It would also make sense to shop at the designer outlets, rather than on Fifth Ave. Emily had mastered the art of putting up appearances long ago. From the very first day she arrived in New York, with just $200 in her fake Gucci wallet and her sister's hand-me-down designer clothes... she knew she needed to use smoke and mirrors to "get to the top" of the food chain.

She placed a pink candle in one of the cupcakes she ordered from her favorite bakery and closed her eyes.

"Happy ten-year anniversary," she whispered aloud. It was ten years to the day since she first arrived in New York to set up her business, Find My Companion. It had been labor of love. And now it was a local "hot spot" for wealthy singletons to find their soul mates. Or, a date for an upcoming event. A lot of her clients were celebrities; actors, NBA players, the occasional Wall Street journalist. Word of mouth brought new business in, but keeping up with the image of a money-rich, successful company hit Emily's platinum cards hard. What did she have to show for it? Matthew's words echoed around her mind like a tin can rolling down an empty alleyway. *What do you know about love?*

A full week had passed since that conversation with the investor. Emily's new plan was going perfectly well. David had endured several dates that did not turn out as well as he hoped. He was primed and ready to be introduced to the *allure* stage of her plan. All she needed to do was convince David that *she* was perfect for him. Once they were officially together, she would call the investors, open up her business in LA, and move to the sunny state of California.

She needed a fresh start. Moving to LA was just as

much about being by the sea as it was about expanding her business. Was she going for domination in the match-making world? No. She just needed to get out of the city and be free from the debts dragging her down. With the raving success of her LA office, she'll be debt-free. Then she could let David go, to find his true love, and she'll live happily ever after... alone. Or maybe she'd get a little dog to carry around in her handbag.

With the vision clear in her mind, Emily opened her eyes and blew out the candle. At precisely the same moment, her phone rang.

***

The dark of night blanketed across the city, illuminated by embers of light from the streetlamps, and blurred by the pouring rain. Emily strained her eyes to catch a glimpse of an approaching vehicle as she waited under the covered doorway.

After a few anxious minutes, the damp, cold evening air chilled Emily to the bone. A black limousine pulled up beside her.

A short gentleman, wearing a full black tux and carrying an umbrella got out of the driver's side and walked over to Emily.

"Ms. Stewart." He touched the front of his driver's hat. "I am Henry," he said, holding out his arm for her to take.

Emily slid her arm through the crook of his elbow and clutched onto the cotton jacket, careful not to snag the fabric with her long, painted nails.

At close proximity, Emily could see lines along his forehead and greying sideburns sticking out from under his hat.

"Nice to meet you," Emily said as politely as she could. Henry opened up an oversized umbrella and held it above their heads as they walked across the path to the limousine.

"Mr. Marks is expecting you." He opened the door and Emily stooped down to enter.

Emily had been in a limousine before, on more than one occasion, in fact. But this was not just a limousine with fancy leather interior and champagne glasses propped up on little tables. This limousine had two large armchairs facing a flat screen TV with an expensive-looking surround sound system.

"Oh, this is fancy!" Emily said as she sidled past the minibar and collapsed into the armchair. The leather squeaked as it stretched to support her weight and cushioned her slim frame.

"New car?" she asked Henry, his head appeared in the doorway as he bent over to smile at her.

"Quite new."

Emily nodded with approval as she looked at her surroundings. "It's got that new car smell." She flashed Henry a charming smile; he nodded and closed the door. No expenses were spared on the interior, Emily noted as she eyed the plush carpeted flooring and the piano black marble edging.

The engine started and only the sound of a faint rumble entered the cabin. As the limousine pulled away, Emily settled back into her comfy seat and fastened the seat belt.

"This is luxury," she said aloud and proceeded to daydream for the entire journey. As the car came to a gentle stop, Emily peered through the dark glass.

The Marks Hotel towered over the city street.

Of course, David is staying here, Emily mused. She craned her neck to look up at the building. It looked like a venetian palace with decorative pillars along the front. It stood out in the contemporary streets of New York. Such was the Marks Hotel brand. Anyone would know a Marks Hotel based on the architecture alone.

Robert stood with his hands clasped together and waited for Emily by the front doors. He inclined his head at her as she approached.

"Hello Robert," Emily said as he held open the glass door for her to enter. Emily walked inside with her head held high and shoulders back. She knew the game… the expectations.

"Ms. Stewart," he said in acknowledgement.

Do I hear a hint of disdain in his voice?

"Please call me Emily," she offered graciously.

Robert offered a small smile in return. They walked along the marble flooring in silence and turned to a doorway that looked like it led to a service area.

Robert held up his wrist to a black electronic pad on the side of the door. At the sound of a click, the heavy door swung open and he stood beside it, patiently waiting.

Emily peered through before taking a step. It wasn't a dirty alleyway, nor a service cupboard, but a private room with a red Persian rug overlaying a gold-colored carpet. A set of French chairs and brocade couches were assembled around the rug and a glass coffee table stood in the center. A set of golden doors hung proudly to the right.

"If you follow me, I'll take you up to Mr. Marks," Robert said formally as he strolled over to the golden doors. He held up his wrist to a scanner and a shrill ping filled the air. The double doors opened up to an elevator.

Cool. Very cool.

Emily concealed a grin with her hand as she waltzed into the elevator.

"So, Robert, how long have you been body-guarding David?' Emily said in an attempt to strike up a friendly conversation.

Bodyguarding? What the heck? Why did I say that?

She grinned sheepishly at Robert, who remained silent as the elevator started to move. The heavy silence in the air indicated David's bodyguards like to keep a professional distance. With her at least. Point taken, she remained quiet as the elevator slowly made its way up to the top floor. Interestingly, there was only one button; it had a picture of a house engraved on it.

The elevator pinged and the golden plated doors rolled back to reveal a small white lobby. Emily walked up to the white door and looked back to see Robert still standing in the elevator.

"Thank you, Robert."

And with that, Robert was gone and she and David were alone. *Play it cool, Emily.*

David smiled warmly at her, his almond shape eyes creased, and his cheekbones became more defined.

"Hmm, I smell steak," Emily said, then walked into the penthouse suite. She stole a few glances to take in the room. Across from the door was an entire wall of glass windows overlooking the city, and to her side a spiral staircase with plush carpet and marble handrails climbed toward the impossibly high ceiling, making David look like an average-sized person, instead of the

6'4" giant he was. Even with her five-inch heels, she still didn't come up to his shoulders.

"I love sunflowers." She ran her fingers along the edges of the bright yellow sunflowers decorating the glass dining table already set with china. David closed the door and followed her.

"I didn't know that."

"You sure? You've not been looking me up online to find out all my weaknesses?"

David laughed and his cheeks flushed.

This is going to be easier than I thought, Emily mused.

"Your timing is perfect. I just had these prepared." David held out his hand and gestured for Emily to take a seat.

"I thought you said you were looking at a plate of food earlier?"

David's forehead reddened as he grinned. "Ah well, these are new…." He lifted the dome covers to reveal two sizzling steak dinners.

Emily took a seat at the table and inhaled. "It smells delicious."

David poured their drinks and took his seat across the table—obscured by the large sunflowers sitting in the middle of the table.

"So this is what it's like to be on a blind date."

Emily covered her mouth as she burst out laughing at the sight of the flowers seemingly talking to her. She heard the jarring sound of a chair scraping across the floor as David's face came back into view, towering over her.

"I'll move these," he said sheepishly. He stooped down and picked up the crystal vase and carried it over to the kitchen. Emily watched the light refract off the crystal and sparkle on the red granite worktop.

"So, this is a date?" Emily asked with a teasing smile as David returned to his seat.

Lines creased around David's eyes as he smirked.

"I wonder how Mandy is getting on with Joffrey?" Emily mused as she picked up her knife and fork. She cut into the fillet steak and brown juices flooded the plate.

David made a humming sound; Emily looked up at him to see him eating his steak with a look of total concentration.

"Why are you chewing that like it's a chunk of an old boot?"

A flash of realization crossed his face and David raised his napkin to his mouth as he swallowed. "I instructed the chef to cook the steak well-done, so not to cause offence."

He did that for me?

"My ex-boyfriend wouldn't even hold the door open for me, let alone burn his steak." Emily picked up her glass and took a sip. A rush of fizz and sugar flooded her senses.

"So, tell me about your week," Emily asked, taking the opportunity to dive into her food and let David do all the talking. David's smile faltered and he glanced around the room in an apparent moment of contemplation.

"I think I've eaten more sushi this week than I have in my entire lifetime."

A sickly sensation swirled inside Emily's stomach at his words. She forced a polite smile as she silently chewed a piece of asparagus.

"The first date… Judy," he began carefully as he stared up at the giant chandelier gleaming above their heads. "She was nice. Only problem is, I think she would make a better wife for my dad."

Emily swallowed and shook her head with her brows raised. "You never said anything about age."

"Yes, but I didn't expect to be set up with someone who is nearly double my age."

Emily suppressed the urge to laugh.

Judy had been on her list for years, a serial dater with no ability to settle down and commit to one person. She was a well-known actress in the 70s, and despite her mature years, acted like a giggly school girl when around people. "Age is just a number, don't you think?"

"That's not all," David said firmly as he sat up straighter. "She only wanted to talk about herself."

"That's what you do on a first date, talk about yourself."

David inclined his head with a grimace. "But her voice—" He stopped, apparently unable to bring himself to say anything offensive.

Emily hummed softly, knowing exactly what he meant. At first, she thought the high-pitched squeal was part of the act when she was in Hollywood. Yet, every phone call with her resulted in a blinding headache.

"Right, so you like a woman who is close to your age, doesn't talk about herself, and has a low voice. This information is helpful," Emily reeled off, in an attempt to sound professional.

"She can talk about herself," David added quickly. "I just prefer a more evenly balanced conversation."

"What about your next date, with—"

"Lola."

"Yes, that's right, the international accountant."

David snorted as he took a bite of his food. "In complete contrast, she didn't speak."

"At all?"

"No, just silence. I asked her questions and she didn't even respond."

"Ah yes, I forgot to mention that she's selectively

mute."

"What!"

"David Marks, do not tell me you discriminate against people with a mental illness?"

"You didn't tell me she had a condition! That would have been helpful... I assumed she hated me."

Emily dabbed her mouth and surveyed David for a moment. The two of them locked eyes and shared an unspoken conversation. Emily was not sure what was being said exactly, but she knew something was happening. The way his cheek dimpled at her, and his eyes narrowed. For a second, she wondered if the game was over. Could he see right through her? Did he know she had set him up? Her panicked thoughts were interrupted by the sound of an elderly woman's voice echoing around the suite.

"David, are you there, David?"

As if he were struck by a bolt of lightning, David scrambled to his feet and gestured for Emily to keep quiet. Alarmed by this personality shift, Emily sat perfectly still and watched David clear his throat and march off into another room.

"Grandmother, how are you feeling today?" his voice trailed off as he disappeared behind a door. Emily crossed her arms and slumped back in her chair. Was this the terminally ill grandmother? Her fragile voice boomed out of the speakers around the suite.

Emily wondered what to do. Should she discretely see herself out and call David later? Or stick around and see how this plays out. Maybe the call wouldn't be long? A couple of awkward minutes passed, and Emily unfolded her arms and finished the rest of her drink.

"Is this your wife, David?"

Emily nearly choked on her drink as she looked frantically around. On the wall behind her, a flat screen TV over the top of a fireplace revealed the close-up of an old woman's face. The elderly woman squinted, and her wrinkled face broke out into a gleeful smile. Emily whipped round in her chair and got to her feet.

"I'm sorry, can you see me?" she blurted out in shock. She glanced back at the sound of hurried foot-steps to see David staring at her with a crazed expression on his face. She frowned at him.

"What do I do?" she mouthed at him. David's fake smile grew as he waved at the TV across the room.

"Sorry, Grandmother, I forgot the TVs are linked," he said formally.

"Come closer, dear, I want to get a good look at you, old eyes, you see."

Emily's sense of panic evaporated as an idea dawned on her. *This is too perfect.* She straightened her black dress and twirled on the spot to look at the TV screen.

"Oh! You must be David's grandmother! He talks so much about you," Emily said in a charming voice as she marched over to the fireplace with her shoulders back and head held high. She ignored the sharp intake of breath from behind her and flicked her hair back confidently as David's grandmother made a noise of approval.

"That's nice, dear. On the contrary, David has told me nothing about you. Tell me, what is your name?"

"I'm his little secret, Emily Stewart." She reached out her hand to David, who stumbled forward with an endearing dumfounded expression. She grabbed his arm and placed her hand on his chest, her fingers glided across the cotton shirt.

"Emily, what is it you do?"

Emily exchanged looks with David for a breath, then tucked a strand of hair behind her ear.

"I'm a business owner here in New York, looking to branch out into LA actually." She glanced at David again, wondering when he was going to step in and take control of the situation like the leader he was. Yet, he appeared to be like a deer stuck in headlights.

"Well, I'm glad to finally meet—" David's grandmother broke into a wheezing coughing fit. The camera jolted up and down and Emily could just make out the sight of an IV stand in the background.

"Grandmother, are you all right? Do you need

something?" David snapped out of his stunned silence. His grandmother came back into normal view and she pressed a tissue to her thin lips.

"I'm moving the date of my party to next week." Her voice was weak, and her pale skin glistened with sweat.

"Next week? You can't—"

"It's my birthday and I can do what I please, David. I am most-anxious to meet you, Emily. I'll have John send the details across."

Emily wrapped her arms around David and squeezed as she offered a gracious smile, he stiffened against her touch.

"We're both looking forward to it, don't worry," she said with a beaming smile.

"I best go, this phone is heavy, and the nurses say I'm not supposed to be making calls."

"Okay, Grandmother, we will see you soon. Rest up." David shrugged out of Emily's grasp and raised a control to turn the TV off. The screen transformed back into a mirror. Emily grinned sheepishly at David as he turned to give her a look of bewilderment. Had she just crossed a line? Was she really so desperate to drag a sick grandmother into the situation? She bit her lip and watched David drag his hand across his brow.

"So... we're married now?"

CHAPTER FOUR

Negotiations

David cradled his favorite mug in his hands and stared at the piping hot chocolate while Emily paced the room.

"What did you do?" he said, dazed.

"What I had to," Emily snapped. She stopped pacing and stood with her hands on her hips. "What else was I supposed to say? 'Oh, hi there, I'm the woman who is trying to find David a fake wife.' Yeah, like that would be any better." Her usually straightened hair was beginning to curl at the ends and fanned out wildly across her shoulders. David couldn't help but notice how fitted her black dress was; the way it sat snug on her hips sent his imagination running as she ranted.

Stop it. Listen to her.

"… on the screen and she could see me, it's not like you were even saying anything."

She had a point. The shock of seeing his grandmother deteriorating so fast threw him back. Her usually tanned complexion had become ashen grey since the last time he saw her. Then she started talking to Emily… David inwardly sighed. She was astute and quick on her feet. When she wrapped her arms around him, the scent of her perfume intoxicated his senses and he became distracted by the heat of her body pressed up against his.

"You do realize what you've done, though?" David placed the mug on the glass coffee table in front of him. "You've introduced yourself to my family as my wife." He looked across the room at Emily and studied her expression. Her eyes were guarded, but the twitch in the corners of her mouth gave her away. "You think this is funny?"

Emily exploded into a fit of laughter as she bent over and clutched her stomach.

"Yes."

The sound of her musical laugh softened David's heart and he stared at her, grinning at the sight of her cheeks flushing as she hyperventilated. His eyes lingered on her red plump lips and he licked his instinctively. Her hazel eyes twinkled, and David was overcome with the urge to race over to her, grab her, and kiss her. His body wilfully obeyed, and before his brain could tell him not to, he found himself on his feet. He must have given Emily a look of intensity because she stopped laughing abruptly and stood up straight, staring at him with wide eyes.

"Are you okay?" She stepped back hesitantly, her reaction stopping him in his tracks.

"I was going to kiss you."

You sound like an idiot. Why did you say that?

Emily opened her mouth and closed it again as she played with her brown hair. David couldn't decide if she was considering the idea or planning her escape. It was the first time he had seen her look unsure. She always acted confident and feisty, the way she swayed her hips and held her shoulders back, further accentuating her curves. The image sent a rush of heat through him and his body tingled. He licked his lips again as he stood immobile.

"So, you want to kiss me?" Her voice was low and silky now, and David clenched his fists, digging his nails into the palms of his hands. He swallowed.

"Yes." His voice sounded alien, like someone was speaking for him. The tingling faded to a numbing sensation; he could no longer feel his arms, or the pain of his nails pressing into his skin. He supposed they should talk about their current predicament. It was a serious situation. But in that moment, his brain forbade him to think about it. Emily was there, looking dangerously tempting and biting her lip, indicating she might share the same thoughts.

Before David could think about anything else, Emily moved forward in a flash and by the time his brain could catch up, his arms were wrapped around her. Emily's hands ran up and down his back. She could barely reach his shoulders, so he stooped down and lifted her up; her body pressed tightly against his. Her head was now above his, her mouth hovering a couple of inches away. Emily closed the gap and their mouths collided and moved in unison. All sensation came crashing back. David spun Emily around and lowered her onto the couch as they kissed. Her hands roamed and the warmth of her mouth against his lips sent vibrations through his body. Minutes later, the two broke apart, panting and breathless. David's head was buzzing, as if he just took a shot of adrenaline. Emily was biting her lip again as her eyes glinted devilishly in the amber lighting. As David leaned in for another kiss, a vibration on his thigh jolted him out of the moment.

"Sorry." He pulled away from Emily and retrieved the phone from his pocket, glancing at the display.

"Oh no," he murmured, seeing the message.

Grandmother's blown up the family phone line, I see.

"Do you need to take that?"

He looked up from his phone to the gorgeous woman sitting next to him and turned his phone off.

"Not now. Let's just have this evening together."

He loosened his blue tie and undid the top button of his shirt. Emily raised her brows at him.

"What are you doing?"

Her words fell like rocks in the pit of his stomach and he promptly stopped moving. Staring into her eyes, he saw the same heat he knew was reflected in his. Cautiously, he lifted his hand and caressed her cheek, leaning in for another kiss. She obliged. This time their exchange was slow and tender.

David felt Emily's hand press against his chest, but instead of it roaming, she gently pushed him back. He looked down to see wet eyes she was trying to conceal.

Is she crying?

"I'm sorry." She appeared to be wrestling with her thoughts. "I think I've been leading you on, and that's not fair."

David stood up too and straightened his shirt. "You are giving mixed signals." He wiped his mouth and looked down at the faint smudge of lipstick staining his fingertips. Then looked up to see Emily straightening her dress.

"I want you to know this wasn't what I planned."
She crossed her arms and looked at him furtively.

It wasn't what I planned, either. But I'm not complaining.

David chewed the inside of his lip as he eyed Emily
carefully. Her brows furrowed as she looked downcast
with her shoulders hunched. David wondered if she
was already regretting their heat-of-the-moment
exchange.

"It's okay," David said in an attempt to be
reassuring.

Emily's eyes snapped up. "What do you want to
do? I'm sure we can stop this before the news gets out."
She wrung her hands and looked wildly around the
room, almost as if expecting David's grandmother to
pop up on the TV again.

David scratched the bristles along his jawline. The
night was wearing on and based on the messages he
received, there were already questions to answer. What
was the best course of action? Call his sick grandmother and tell her it was a ruse? But then it would
raise the question of who Emily really was, and what
she was doing in his penthouse, alone. He would be
forced to confess that he had never been married, and
the consequences of doing that were costly.

The doorbell interrupted his thoughts.

"Yes," David called out from the living room,
looking past Emily who had walked over to the break-

fast bar. Robert stood in the front doorway with his hands clasped together.

"Sorry for the intrusion, sir." David gestured for him to come into the room. "We have a situation downstairs," he whispered, nearing the sofa.

David studied his face. Robert's eyes shot to Emily briefly and he cleared his throat. Whatever it was he wanted to say, he did not feel comfortable sharing it with Emily in the room.

"Emily, would you mind—"

"Yes, of course, I'll see myself out." Emily placed her mug on the breakfast bar and walked through to the front entryway. Her heels clicked against the marble flooring, and David stole a glance at her figure as she sauntered away. He turned back to Robert.

"Talk to me." Robert relaxed his shoulders and stood upright.

"Your father is here."

A sense of dread flooded David's veins and the hairs on his forearms stood on end. Before he could say anything, the sound of loud voices echoed around the room as the front door opened.

"So, you're David's secret wife? When I heard that you were here, I had to come over and see...." David's father strolled in with Emily's arm linked with his and rested his other hand over hers in the crook of his elbow.

Mr. Marks was never seen in public wearing anything other than a designer suit. His perfectly buffed shoes shined in the lighting and squeaked against the floor. He sported his usual side parting and a neatly trimmed silver moustache. He, too, towered over Emily, though he was slightly shorter than David. However, having a height disadvantage did not deter Mr. Marks from reminding his son who was boss.

Emily held a beaming smile, but he noted her eyes were wide and frantic.

"David. Where have you been hiding this wife of yours?"

Robert offered an apologetic smile at David and inclined his head. He resisted the urge to glare back. Instead, he looked over to Emily, who was staring at him with intent. He didn't need her to speak; he could hear her screaming inside his head.

How do we get out of this?

CHAPTER FIVE

An Unexpected Guest

Emily wrestled with her thoughts as she maintained a perfectly poised stance, still holding onto the arm of Mr. Marks. The look on David's face would usually have made Emily laugh, but this situation was far from amusing. What could have been corrected as a simple case of misunderstanding, had now developed into a growing web of lies. She was getting in too deep, she never planned to get family involved.

What do you want to do?

David's jaw jutted out, his smile tense. Following an awkward moment, where no one made a move, Robert excused himself and vacated the suite. Emily watched him with envy.

"I apologize for arriving here unannounced. I just got off the phone with your grandmother and had to come over." Mr. Marks' voice was serene and charming. There was a gentleness about him that threw Emily off guard. She clung onto him as if his calming nature were a magnet and she had no choice but to remain by his side. Despite the bizarre situation, she wondered if everything would sort itself out after all.

"Yes, we were caught by surprise earlier, I had been hoping to wait—"

"Not inviting your family to the nuptials is one thing, David," Mr. Marks interjected, "but to keep me from meeting my newest daughter-in-law is most inappropriate." He turned and gazed adoringly at her, as if he were her loving father. A pang of guilt ached within her midriff, and she momentarily lowered her eyes from his.

"It's my fault." She pulled her arms away as if breaking the spell he had over her and walked over to David. "I insisted we kept it quiet." She took David's clammy hand in hers and squeezed.

"Would you like me to get you a drink?" David asked as if on autopilot. Mr. Marks waved a hand as he strolled into the kitchen area and took out a glass from one of the cabinets.

"It's all right, I can help myself," he replied as he poured himself a drink. David and Emily took the opportunity to exchange looks.

"Play along?" Emily whispered to him. David nodded his head ever so slightly and cleared his throat. Emily turned to Mr. Marks who had settled himself down on the couch. The same couch she and David made out on just minutes earlier. She bit her quivering lip.

"I was just explaining to Mr. Marks—"

"Please call me Charles."

"Right, Charles… I was on my way out to the store," Emily added as she turned back to look at David.

"And I said that was preposterous at this time of night. You have staff to help you with errands."

Charles took a sip of his drink and surveyed the couple over his glass. Emily stood frozen on the spot, her hand squeezing David in a death grip.

"You're quite right," David said as he tugged on her hand and they walked over to join Charles in the seating area. "Emily likes to have autonomy. Neverthe-less, I am trying to persuade her to delegate responsi-bilities."

David and Charles continued to have a polite conversation about the lifestyle they had been accus-tomed to, and Emily found herself daydreaming.

Private jet planes, security staff, dieticians, a personal chef, driver, shrink... Emily snapped out of her thoughts at the sound of her name.

"Emily, are you feeling well?"

She blinked several times and looked from Charles to David with a quizzical look. She caught a glimpse of movement in the corner of her eye and turned to see Charles place his empty glass on the coffee table and stand up.

"I think it best that I let you to two rest. I apologize for interrupting your evening." He held out his hand for David to shake. Then he turned to Emily, deep lines formed around his eyes and his cheeks dimpled as he smiled. "It was charming to meet you, Emily. I look forward to spending more time with you next week."

"Yes, next week! So much to prepare!" Emily said heartily as the three of them walked to the door. David clapped Charles on the back of his shoulders and opened the door for him.

"Good night," he said as he turned on the spot and left the penthouse.

"Cheerio."

David closed the door and looked at Emily incredulously.

"Cheerio?"

Emily creased over with laughter.

"I'm sorry," she said. "I have no idea where that came from." David walked across to the breakfast bar.

"Our drinks have gone cold. What do you say we grab a fresh hot chocolate and talk about our next move?"

Emily sighed. Her ankles were aching, and her neck was sore. She longed to take off her tight dress and get into her snuggly pajamas. But unfortunately, David was right. They had to talk.

"Lovely, but just one thing; do you mind if I take my shoes off? These heels are pinching my toes like crazy."

E mily stared up at the white ceiling of the bedroom in her downtown apartment. Her shoes were cast across the bedroom floor, along with her black dress, and she spread out like a starfish on a king-size bed finally in her favorite pair of pajamas. The sun was starting to creep up into the sky and an orange glow flooded the room as Emily replayed the events of the evening.

She was the new Mrs. Marks—unofficially. Surely, this was the best outcome she could have hoped for.

Then, why do I feel so sick?

She rolled over to her side and clutched her

stomach as she watched the hands on her bedside clock tick. All her problems were now solved. She could call Matthew and explain to the investors that she was married after all. It would be easy to explain that David, in his high profile position, wanted to keep their marriage private.

Then, I'll open up a new office in LA and live my new life following an amicable "divorce."

She narrowed her eyes and scrunched up her nose at the thought. That plan had several ethical flaws.

Or did it? The investors refusal to work with her because of her marital status was downright discrimination. And David was in a sticky situation. His family thought he was married—that wasn't Emily's doing. *He* told that lie. She only manipulated his dating experiences. The somewhat unfortunate chain of events that followed allowed her to step in and take on the role as his wife. She was doing him a favor.

Though David had made it clear in their initial interview he was looking for love. Not just a woman to take on the title of wife.

Emily ruined that.

She rubbed her temples and closed her eyes against the throbbing migraine beginning to form. She had fooled David into thinking that she was doing him a favor, but he didn't know her motivation was not entirely altruistic.

He's so sweet and kind… He shouldn't be with a person like me.

The man had his steak burnt to a crisp because she hated the sight of blood. *Who does that for a person they've barely met?* He spoke to her in a way that made her feel like an equal—that there was not a huge financial rift between them.

His grandmother looked so frail and weak, struggling to hold the camera as she spoke on the phone. Then there was Charles, who had in ten minutes, shown her more warmth than her own father had in her entire lifetime. She rolled onto her back and crossed her arms.

With a frown her mind replayed the conversation with David over hot chocolate. He'd offered to tell his family the truth. He would end the charade and own up to the fact he was not married. Perhaps that was the right thing to do and the best for David. He could be free of any drama and they would go on with their lives. After all, if he knew the truth of her intentions, he would be justifiably furious and probably never want to see her again.

But then she remembered *that kiss*. She brushed her lips with her fingertips and swallowed. The glint in his eyes as he tugged at his tie and unbuttoned his shirt. Emily turned and pressed her grinning face into a pillow. They had only been in the same room together twice. *Twice, Emily! Have you no boundaries?*

Despite knowing that it was probably for the best if David told his family the truth, she wanted to see him again. Maybe she could have it all? Help David with his family situation, win over the heart of the investors... *and their wallets.* She grinned. And find... *dare I think it? Love.*

CHAPTER SIX

MRS. MARKS

D avid stood anxiously with his hands clasped together as he shifted his weight. A string quartet played a whimsical Mozart melody, and the guests, dressed in their best clothes, were talking in their seats. The chapel was full of pink and yellow roses adorning the end of the pews, and a huge array of lilies sat on the table at the front of the chapel. David looked over to Joffrey, who was feeding Mandy shrimp. She giggled and adoringly stroked his red beard as she chewed. A sea of faces he did not recognize sat in the crowd, and FBI agents stood at the doors.

A moan caught his attention, and he looked back to see the female priest eating a steak dinner. The music stopped and David *watched the priest cough and splutter as she hurried to finish chewing her food.*

"Please stand," she said with her mouth full of steak. David looked at the wooden chapel doors that were now thrown open, and a beam of sunlight flooded his vision. A figure appeared in the light and as it moved forward, he saw her. The chiffon mermaid dress shimmered and dazzled. Emily was walking with Jaqueline by her side. Her dark hair was tied back into a sleek bun. The bouquet in her hands was made up entirely of sunflowers. She beamed at him, her eyes twinkling. David swallowed and took her hand in his when she reached him.

"I love you," she mouthed. When she opened her mouth though, a forked tongue flipped out and withdrew as quickly as it appeared. David frowned and shook his head. Then he looked back at Emily to find he was face to face with the biggest snake he had ever seen.

"I do," the snake hissed.

David jolted awake and panted as he lay in the darkness. His heart pounded in his chest as he covered his face with his hands. He sat up and the covers fell away from his chest, allowing the cold air to blast against his bare skin. He shivered.

"Omeba, turn the A/C off," he said through a yawn and rubbed the sleep out of his eyes.

"Air conditioning is now off. What else can I assist you with?" a robotic voice echoed around the room. David dragged his legs out of bed and hunched over with his elbows resting on his knees. He yawned again and dragged a hand through his coarse hair.

"Open the blinds." The crisp grey blinds rotated open and a weak stream of sunlight filtered into the room. The sky was almost blue with a tinge of pink as the sun crept slowly into the sky. A new day was born, and David already had a lot on his mind. The previous day had been one of the longest of his life and he was still reeling from it. A vibration on his nightstand jarred him from his thoughts.

"Joffrey, how was your date?"

A resounding groan echoed out of the speakers and David tried to suppress a laugh. "I owe you for that," he added.

"You don't owe me anything." Joffrey's voice was gruff and defeated. "You said it, remember? It's my job to protect you."

"What's the news?" David crossed his room and pulled a white towel from the linen closet.

"I got a message to call you."

David draped the towel over his shoulder.

"Right, I'll send you an address to collect Ms. Stewart. I need you to accompany her for the time being." The room was still and quiet in response. "Joffrey?"

"I'm sorry—I'm not sure I understand. Am I going on another date for you?"

David rolled his eyes.

"No. Ms. Stewart and I have an arrangement, and I need you to be her security until I say so."

"Yes, sir."

David scratched the bristles on his chin.

"How did you end things with Mandy?" he asked, flashes of his nightmare crossed his mind. He recoiled at the thought of Joffrey feeding Mandy shrimp.

"You won't be hearing from her again," Joffrey said in a firm voice. Sensing that there was more to the story Joffrey didn't want to share, David nodded to himself.

"Right, good luck with Ms. Stewart, and keep her safe."

David had a quick shower and carefully shaved as his mind wandered off. Having a woman pretend to be his wife was not what he had in mind. He berated himself for getting into this mess in the first place. If he just had more time... if Grandmother had not written such a ridiculous clause in her will.... Emily was doing him a massive favor. But why? He wondered what was in it for her? He thought it would have been harder to get her on his side.

David dressed in a blue Armani suit and gelled his hair to tame the curls threatening to form. He surveyed his appearance in the floor length mirror and made a murmur of approval.

"Omeba," he said as he pulled on his socks.

"Yes, Mr. Marks."

"What do I have on the agenda today?" He walked over to his walk-in closet and grabbed a pair of brown leather shoes.

"You are meeting your father for breakfast. Lunch with Emily Stewart. And your flight leaves this evening." Before David could process, he noticed his phone vibrating on the bed. He picked it up and smiled at the name flashing on the screen. "Hi there," he said charmingly.

"What is Joffrey doing here?"

"We talked about this last night."

"And I told you that I didn't need anyone to protect me."

"Emily, if you're going to be my wife…."

"Fake wife," she corrected. David clenched his jaw.

"Then you're going to need to look the part. There's no way I would let my wife walk around without security."

Emily seemed unable to argue. When they ended their conversation, her question echoed in his mind.

"And I suppose you expect me to come and live with you too, then?"

David held his breath as he considered it. How did neither of them think to discuss their living arrangements? He grinned as he remembered why. She was too busy distracting him. She sat, curled up on the couch, with her feet tucked under her legs and her hair fanned out over her shoulders. He said something funny, and her chest heaved up and down as she laughed in response. She touched his arm briefly and threw her head back with a chuckle after saying something witty. Their time could have been better spent exchanging ideas on how they were going to navigate the next few weeks. But it was getting late and his brain had been sluggish.

They agreed to meet for lunch the next day. Emily said she had to go into the office for the morning and deal with some "loose ends." Whatever they were.

David was able to hand over his work to his team for the rest of the month. Yet, being like his dad, he preferred to wear smart attire even when he wasn't going to work. He looked at himself in the mirror again, this time wearing his shoes. *Is this too formal?* he wondered. Both times he met Emily, she wore a figure-hugging outfit with high heels. He figured if he rolled up in a limousine wearing denim, he'd look under-dressed for the occasion. Something about his outfit did look wrong, though. He pulled off his tie and unbuttoned the top of his grey shirt. Then he relaxed his shoulders and pointed to himself in the mirror, practicing a smoldering look on his face. He broke into a grin.

That's more like it.

David pressed a hand to his stomach as it growled angrily at him. And as if his kitchen staff had spider senses, the doorbell rang, then a small woman pushing a trolley laden full of food entered his bedroom suite.

"Breakfast. Thank you, Marie," David said as he glanced at his watch, his father would be arriving soon. He popped a mini croissant into his mouth. Having traveled to most countries across the globe, David had enjoyed many traditional breakfasts. However, he was most happy with a continental. Nothing settled a grumbling stomach as well as a buttered croissant and glass of orange juice.

David sat in the empty penthouse and peered around the oversized room with his brows knitted together. Despite having a team of staff waiting to jump into action on his command, David was always alone. He'd attended a private boys' school in London and having no inclination to sneak off with the other classmates to the girls' school two blocks away, David never had a girlfriend. Leaving school only posed more obstacles in his way to finding a companion. Girls roamed around in packs, it was near impossible to get to speak to one alone, and no one taught him how. By the time he reached adulthood, David's family wealth was well-known, and he had Joffrey and Robert assigned as his security, to follow his every move. It made it difficult to have a casual drink with a new girl, or even approach one to ask on a date. There was online dating... But his father strictly advised against it. The question remained: How does a billionaire find a date? He inwardly chuckled at the thought of billboard posters along the freeway with his portrait and the words, Who Wants to Date a Billionaire? across the top.

Harold, a school friend, had taken over his father's business in the entertainment industry. The glitz and glamor of Hollywood demanded a lot of media attention. It wasn't long before his friend was known as one of the richest producers in the industry. Apparently, Emily introduced him to his wife, Julie. The two had been happily married for five years and to this day, Harold continued to praise Emily for her matchmaking skills.

Emily, however, had set David up with the oddest women. Why had she not found him a "Julie"? Were women like that so rare? Were June, the geriatric actress, and Mandy, the fortune teller, the best she could offer him?

He clenched his jaw. But that wasn't part of the plan anyway. And besides... had he already found his future wife? Had she been sitting right in front of him that first day he'd met her? He wondered if that was why the other women felt so wrong. No one compared to Emily. The week had been wasted, when he could have spent that time getting to know her.

David's mind ran away with him as he fantasized about Emily, and he lost track of time. He berated himself and decided to leave. Grinning like a fool and letting his staff tell his father he'd changed plans, he made his way down the elevator to the lobby.

CHAPTER SEVEN

FLY ME TO THE MOON

"Jaqueline, can you come in, please?" The white door to Emily's office opened slowly and Jaqueline stuck her head through.

"Get me the Faulkner file when you're done, dollface." Julian's voice trailed into the office. With her cheeks flushed, Jaqueline looked quizzically around the room until her wide eyes rested on Emily, who was sitting on the couch sipping herbal tea.

"What can I get you, Ms. Stewart?" Jaqueline asked in her fake-polite voice. Emily motioned for her to sit on the couch. She watched Jaqueline chew her lips and fiddle with the ties hanging down from her wrists. Her white ribbed shirt laced up on the sleeves and neckline; it was quite trendy. Her pencil denim skirt hung past her knees and she wore a pair of brown faded cowboy boots. All in all, not a bad look, she just needed a checked necktie and her hair in a braid and she'd be ready for a rodeo. Jaqueline sat down next to Emily; she was so slight that the couch barely shifted under her weight.

"How old are you, Jaqueline?" Emily asked softly. Jaqueline stared back, her eyes like saucers and her mouth hanging open.

"Twenty-one, Ms. Stewart," she said in the smallest voice. Emily could hardly make out the words. Her hands were trembling. She sat like a little lamb waiting to be taken to the slaughterhouse.

Really? Am I that scary? Poor timid thing.

"Are you good at keeping secrets?" Emily asked as she patted her knee. Jaqueline jumped as if struck by a bolt of lightning.

"I—well—um—yes, I think so," she stammered, now on her feet again.

"Great." She needed to let someone in on the situation she'd hatched and now found herself embroiled in with David. She was too busy to nurture friendships and she hadn't seen or spoken to her sister for months. Jaqueline on the other hand, well, she saw her every day and she had the added bonus of knowing where she lived. Who better to divulge your deepest secrets to than your personal assistant who picks up your tampons?

"Sit down, Jaqueline. I need to tell you something. Big. And it needs to stay between us, okay?" Emily said slowly and firmly. Jaqueline's eyes grew even wider and she settled back down in the seat, looking at Emily with a mixture of relief and intrigue.

"Okay, Ms. Stewart, I won't tell a soul, I promise."

Emily stood in the restroom staring at herself in the mirror. She pulled off a few stray hairs from her red sweater and smoothed the wrinkles out of her black trousers. A toilet flushed and one of the cubicle doors opened behind her; she turned to see Jaqueline.

"Did you make the call?"

"Everything is set up," she said as she bent over the sink and washed her hands.

"Good," Emily said as she exhaled. She eyed Jaqueline carefully, watching her delicately dry her hands with a paper towel.

"You can call me Emily, you know."

Jaqueline stopped moving momentarily and her

nostrils flared. Emily couldn't decide if that was a good sign or not.

"Thank you, but I think I prefer Ms. Stewart," she said finally before throwing the used paper towel in the trash. She was so timid, and now she was moody?

What is the deal with this girl?

"You have a bit of a temper, don't you?" Emily rested a hand on her hip as she ran her fingers through her hair.

"I'm sorry." Jaqueline's shoulders slumped in defeat. "I feel better calling you Ms. Stewart… seeing as I've called you that for years."

"Years? How long have you worked here?"

"Three years."

"Didn't you go to college?"

Jaqueline's nostrils flared again, and her pupils dilated. Emily chewed the inside of her cheek.

Why is she behaving this way? I'm her boss.

"I took an internship here instead," she said firmly. Emily drummed her fingers on her hip bone and surveyed the girl's determined expression. She was hungry for something. Was it money? Recognition?

"So, you've been here for three years as my personal assistant. Tell me, do you want to work with clients?" As soon as the words left Emily's mouth, Jaqueline's eyes lit up.

"Yes," she said back to her small voice. The two women stood facing each other in silence.

"Right, you know the plan. If this works out, you can expect a promotion."

Jaqueline rocked on the heels of her feet and clasped her hands together her face broke out into a beaming smile.

"Thank you, Ms. Stewart. Thank you."

E mily sat at her desk with her fingers interlocking and resting on her pink notepad. She looked up at the clock and shifted in her chair, uncrossing her ankles and crossing them again nervously. She had managed to keep busy with meetings that morning. Now that she'd met with everyone in her company, she sat at her desk with nothing left to do but wait.

When her yellow phone rang, Emily jumped in her seat and stared at it like it was a bomb. She cleared her throat, straightened her back, and picked up the phone.

"Emily Stewart speaking."

"Hi Emily, it's Matthew." Emily deliberated whether he spoke in a tone that suggested he was happy or politely irritated.

"Ah, thank you for your call Matthew."

"Found yourself a fella already, have you? That was fast."

"Actually, I have a bit of a confession to make."

"Ah. I'm sorry, but you should know that I'm happily married."

"Sorry?" She leaned back in her chair and folded her arms.

"Hmm, you weren't going to confess your undying love for me?"

"I—we've never even met!" Emily spluttered, caught off guard. Mathew chortled down the phone as she chewed her lip and wondered what to say.

"Sorry," he said as he wheezed. "Bad joke, but I couldn't resist."

Emily swallowed and clutched the phone in her hand as she built up the courage to speak again.

"I was not entirely honest with you during our previous conversation."

"Is that so?"

"You see, I like to keep my private life just that, private. When you asked me if I was in a relationship, I was not quite sure how to reply honestly. My husband—"

"You're married?"

"Yes, my husband is very private and stays out of the media."

"Oh, so he's famous? Some hunk Hollywood actor I know?"

"No, no he's not an actor."

"Hmm. All right, well this is interesting. I'll tell you what, let's have dinner and talk about your proposition."

Butterflies flew around in Emily's midriff as a surge of excitement coursed through her veins.

"That is a great idea, I'd be more than happy to—"

"You and your husband, of course. We can arrange a discreet venue, I'm sure."

Emily stared at the wood grain of her desk and froze. "Right. Of course." Panicked, she lost sensation in her arms. "When are you thinking?"

Matthew cleared his throat loudly and hummed. Emily imagined he was scrolling through his calendar.

"I'll have to talk to the other investors and get back to you," he said gruffly. Emily exhaled and wriggled in her chair.

"That's fine. We'll smooth out the details later." She dragged her fingers through her hair and chewed her upper lip. When the call ended, she looked up at the clock to see she was late. As if on cue, the door swung open and Joffrey strolled into the office. His full red beard was straight and smooth, and Emily wondered if he used hair straighteners on it. She smirked at the thought.

"Can I help you?" she asked as Joffrey walked toward her. He stopped on the spot and rolled his shoulders back.

"Yes, I am here to take you to your—" He looked shiftily around the room as if to check for prying ears. "—husband," he added. Emily laughed.

"Okay, Joffrey, thank you. I'll just get my bag."

CHAPTER EIGHT

FLY ME TO THE MOON

"I s this too much?" David asked Robert as he pointed to his bow tie. He was all thumbs, fumbling with his buttons when he got dressed, and he changed his mind on his shirt five times before he settled on a simple light grey one. Robert looked like he was resisting the urge to roll his eyes and gave David an odd smile.

"No," he said, his voice dripping with sarcasm. David typically reminded people to maintain manners and who was the boss... but this was Robert. Joffrey and Robert were like older brothers to David. They knew everything about him, and of all the staff, only they were granted the right of being less formal. Only in private, of course. David pulled on the tie and stuffed it in his pocket.

A black limousine pulled up alongside the gentlemen. David nervously ruffled the front of his dark hair and unbuttoned the top of his shirt. He clamped his jaw as he watched Henry get out of the car and smile at him. David gave him a nod and Henry opened the back door.

Two narrow feet wearing black stilettos stepped out of the car, and he caught sight of a flash of silky-smooth legs, looking tanned next to the ivory cotton skirt that came to the knee. Henry held out his arm and a slender hand reached out. David's mouth was dry as he swallowed and shifted his weight on the spot. He placed his hands in his pockets, then clasped them in front of him, unsure what to do with them. Emily stood up gracefully. Her long hair caught in a gust of wind, flew to the side like she was in a shampoo advertisement. Her big eyes narrowed when she spotted him, but her lips curved into a grin.

"Hello," she said. Her words sent a bolt of excitement through David and he sprung into a hurried walk toward her. He stuck out his hand for her to shake, her eyes lingered on it as if she had never seen a hand before. David dropped it with a laugh and raised his arms and gave her an awkward hug.

"How was your morning?"

Emily placed her hands on her hips and leaned to the side, eyeing the helicopter behind David.

"Boring," she said. "Looks like my day is about to get more interesting though." Joffrey and Robert followed them to the helicopter, but David turned and pressed a finger to his lips in thought.

"I'd like you both to stay here."

Robert and Joffrey exchanged looks. "There's a great coffee shop just down the road. Please wait. We'll be back in a few hours."

He looked around the deserted parking lot and his eyes landed on Emily again. She was a jewel in the desert. She flashed him a grin and her pearly white teeth shone in the sunlight.

"What's for lunch? I'm starving." She slipped her hand through the crook of his arm and the two of them walked to the helicopter. David couldn't help but notice the sheer material of her blouse that revealed the gentle curves of her shoulders and the refined collarbone above the sweetheart neckline. He was ravenous as well—though maybe for something entirely different than food.

He stood beside the helicopter door and held Emily's hand as she climbed inside. "Whatever you want," he said as he followed her inside.

"I'm really craving a Cinnabon." Emily stepped

aside as David closed the door and climbed into the pilot's seat.

"That sounds like a healthy lunch," he mused as he started the engine. He glanced back to see Emily with her mouth hanging open.

"You're flying?"

David turned back to the control and grinned to himself.

"Come and take a seat." He patted on the co-pilot's chair and watched Emily from the corner of his eye as she hesitantly climbed into the seat. He handed her a pair of headphones, then cranked the engine.

"Put these on," he shouted over the sound of the engine. The propeller was spinning loudly and the helicopter rumbled. Emily placed the headphones on her head and David did the same.

"You look so cute," he said, seeing the earphones squishing her cheeks. Emily pulled a face and cocked her head to the side.

"What?" she shouted.

David shook his head and busied himself with the controls.

"Ready?" Not waiting for her reply, he piloted the aircraft up and over New York City. The skyscrapers sparkled in the blazing sunshine and David glanced over at Emily to see her reaction. Her hand flew over and grabbed his leg as she leaned into the window.

David swallowed and focused on keeping the heli-copter in flight, ignoring the pinching sensation of Emily's fingernails digging into his leg. After a few minutes, she pulled her hand away and David caught sight of her cheeks reddening as she bit her lip and looked away. He took a hard right and the helicopter swung to the side; Emily gasped and gripped the bottom of her seat. Her back was straight as a board and her eyes were like saucers, taking in the scenery.

"Do you like it?" he shouted. Emily turned to him and offered a beaming smile. Her face was lit up like a little girl on Christmas day.

"This is AMAZING."

David reached their destination, a large skyscraper with a hidden helipad on the rooftop.

"Wow," Emily said with a big sigh, once the engine stopped running. David wondered if she had been holding her breath. "What a rush!"

"Have you never been in a helicopter before?" David asked as they unfastened their belts and straight-ened their clothes. Emily pulled off her headphones and shook her head.

"I've set up dates for clients before. I know they do helicopter tours of the city and always wanted to do it, but just haven't had the time."

They locked eyes for a moment and just stared at one another. Sitting in such close proximity, David could make out the faint freckles on Emily's cheeks and the shine of her lip gloss invited him in for a kiss. He inhaled nervously. Flurries of excitement grew in his stomach as he considered making a move. What was the hesitation? It was so easy to throw caution to the wind and dive in the night before. Now… in broad daylight, there was something about her guarded eyes and the way she leaned back against the window that had him wondering; maybe she didn't want him to kiss her?

"Shall we get out?" Emily said. David snapped out of his thoughts and nodded. He climbed out of the helicopter and held Emily's hand. She remained perfectly poised as she descended the steps and smoothed her skirt.

"Where are we?"

David motioned for them to walk and Emily linked her arm with his.

"I thought we could eat somewhere private… with a view."

They entered through a steel door and David led Emily down a flight of steps. The hall wrapped around a corner and David raised his watch to a metal grid beside a door. It clicked and the door swung open. When they entered, David craned his neck to get a good look at Emily's reaction.

"Oh."

Her mouth fell open and her eyes widened as she took in the room. David beamed with pride, happy with the response.

"Is this… a ballroom?"

She let go of David's arm and twirled in the center of the huge room. Three large chandeliers hung from the mirrored ceiling and a line of glass windows covered the back wall. The golden sunshine shimmered over Emily's dark hair with her movements and she spread her arms out wide. David had been impressed at how composed she was, yet it was a rush seeing that she had the ability to let her hair down with such enthusiasm.

"It could be a ballroom," he finally said. Realizing he had not yet answered Emily's question. He strolled over to her and offered his hands. She accepted it, and they took a dancing position and waltzed around in circles amongst the circular tables in the hall. A resounding bang had them drop their hands and look at the door.

"So sorry," a petite woman, dressed as a chef walked into the room with a large trolley of food. A group of staff followed. David watched them dress one of the circular tables and set out their meal. He marveled at how fast they were able to work and noticed that no one made eye contact with him.

"Thank you," he said as he motioned for Emily to

take a seat. She gracefully lowered into a chair and smiled up at the staff working around them.

"Thanks, this is great," she said to the chef as she put down a plate of food in front of her. Wild salmon on a bed of brown rice and quinoa with an array of vegetables adorned the plate. Even to David, who was a bigger fan of red meat, salivated at the sight of it. He gestured to the chef.

"Excuse me."

The chef jumped at the sound of David's voice and straightened her hat as she hurried over to him. Her dark narrow eyes were wide with anticipation. David leaned close to her and she clasped her hands together as he whispered into her ear.

"Could you prepare some cinnamon buns for dessert?"

The chef's face broke into a smile and she bowed her head. "Yes, sir,"

David eyed Emily, who had already placed her napkin in her lap and picked up her knife and fork. "You're not waiting around, hey?"

Emily looked up at him after popping a piece of salmon in her mouth, then slumped into her seat with a moan. She closed her eyes and shook her head, with a drunken smile on her face. "I told you," she said between bites. "I'm starving."

David grinned, quite unaware of the steaming

plate of food set before him. He stared at Emily as she made herself comfortable and devoured her meal. It stirred up emotions that he hadn't experienced before; it was a bittersweet sensation. Happiness mingled with sadness. A sense of belonging mixed with regret. He fiddled with his watch and clenched his jaw as his mind battled.

I should tell her the truth and get it over with… but then she'll leave and never speak to me again.

Emily opened her eyes and grinned at him as she chewed, her cheeks bulged like a hamster and her eyes sparkled. David wanted to rush over and scoop her up in his arms, kissing those cheeks and lose himself in her sparkling eyes forever.

She's too good for you, David. If she finds out what you've done, she will never forgive you.

CHAPTER NINE

A GROWING APPETITE

"You've barely touched your food, everything okay?" Emily eyed David suspiciously while dabbing her mouth with her napkin. David averted his eyes and took a sip of his drink, perhaps to avoid answering the question. They ate in silence for a few minutes, when the chef reappeared. She placed on the table a warm plate of cinnamon buns drenched in white icing. Emily licked her lips and grinned at the chef.

"These look delicious."

"Thank you, ma'am." She inclined her head with a slight bow. "I hope they live up to your expectations."

Emily picked up a cinnamon roll and took a bite. A gentle explosion of vanilla and cinnamon delivered on a fluffy bed of pastry sent Emily's senses into a frenzy. She melted into her seat and gave a thumbs up as she made a noise of approval.

"If you don't hurry up and eat, David, I'm going to finish them all," she teased. She shot a charming smile at the chef, who appeared unsure whether to apologize for not making enough or laugh along. She settled on another awkward bow with a faint smile and vacated the room in silence.

"We have a lot to talk about," Emily said as she finished her roll. She picked up her drink and swirled it in the glass absent-mindedly.

"Yes, before we get to that, I have something for you." David shifted in his seat and pulled out a little black box from his pocket. Emily inhaled as she stared at it. He flipped it open and a platinum ring, sporting a diamond the size of an almond, was staring at her.

"David. This is… unexpected."

David shrugged.

"We're married now, might as well fit the part." He lifted up his left hand to show a plain platinum band on his wedding finger. Emily bit her lip to stop herself from grinning, wondering how she didn't notice it before. She reached out and he placed the ring on her finger. She stared at it, surprised at how heavy the diamond weighed on her hand. *I'm going to get mugged on the subway with this rock on my finger.*

"It fits perfectly. How did you know my ring size?" David offered a broad smile with his back straight. Clearly proud of himself.

"I have my secrets," he said, while tapping his nose. Emily wriggled in her seat and rubbed her arms.

"I have a confession to make," she said. David raised his brows as he picked up his knife and fork. Emily glanced out of the huge pane of windows to see the city and took a moment to carefully choose her words. Now, would be a good time to come clean and tell him that she set him up. The dates were manipulated to get him to choose her so she could expand her company.

"Okay, I'm listening," David said, urging Emily to speak. She stared at him intently. His jawline jutted out and his face looked like it had been chiseled by an expert. She wanted to run her fingers along his brow and grab the back of his neck.

"Sorry," she blurted out, heat rising to her face. "What was I saying?" Lightheaded, Emily lost track of her thoughts as she took a sip of her drink to calm down.

"You had a confession for me?"

Emily was blushing fully now. His steady gaze was intense and burned through her soul.

She couldn't do it.

"I like you," she said without thinking. David smirked.

"Thanks."

"No, I mean... I like you." Emily sat up straighter and smoothed her hair. "I know this is an act... I know we haven't known each other very long. But I want you to know that, I feel something," Emily stammered. David continue to stare at her with a look of intensity. She couldn't work out if he was having an inward conversation, or just taking time to register what she was saying. Before David could answer, Emily's phone vibrated.

"Sorry, I should check if that's work," she murmured as she pulled out her phone and glanced at it. It was a text message from Matthew.

"Ah," she said, her stomach tightening. "Are you free tonight? I need a favor."

David nodded. Apparently unable to find his voice.

"I need to go to dinner with my investors, and they want to meet you."

"Me?"

Emily hesitated. *How do I explain this?* "Well, the fact that I'm married may have come up in conversation, and they were keen to meet you."

"Okay, so this is really happening." David puffed his cheeks out and exhaled. Emily smirked as she lifted her left hand up to him; the huge ring twinkled brighter than the chandeliers above their heads.

"Well, yes."

David smirked back.

"Okay. Now if we are to fool anyone that we're a couple, we better get to know each other, fast." Emily picked up another cinnamon roll and grinned. David picked one up too.

"In that case, I think we're going to need more of these."

———

E mily studied her face in the bathroom, looking for flaws. Apart from the faint line between her brows and the corners of her eyes, she could have been mistaken for a twenty-year-old. She curled the last lock of straight hair and plucked out a tiny grey strand. She then stood back and admired her work. Masses of soft brown curls covered her shoulders and fanned out like a mermaid. She tugged on the towel wrapped around her body and held it in place as she trudged into her bedroom wearing her pink bunny slippers. Now that her hair and make-up were perfect, all she had to do was pick an outfit.

What do you wear to a dinner with your fake husband and

potential investors? She eyed a long, figure-hugging nude gown, designed by Vivienne Westwood. It was easily the most expensive item in her wardrobe, but perhaps not the best idea when you're looking to have people invest in your company. She wanted to appear tasteful and accomplished, but didn't scream money. She opted for a pastel pink lace Ted Baker dress. The soft, feminine style worked well with her curly hair and she decided it was the perfect blend between tasteful and yet ordinary. She slipped on the dress and expertly zipped it up, looking like a contortionist with her arms flung back to work the zipper. She ran her hands down the material. The dress hugged her curves and fit like a glove, moving with her easily, as if it were an extra layer of skin. She grabbed her favorite bottle of perfume and sprayed it liberally into the air and walked into the fragrant plume. She tried to remember everything David told her at lunch. Thankfully, after all these years of meeting clients and matchmaking, memory recall became a strength. She was able to collect facts and store them better than anyone.

David was born in London and went to boarding school. His height made him clumsy, and he was known for dropping things or tripping up and was bullied mercilessly for it. High school was better, having made a few close friends and the other students became aware of his family's fortune. Kids would try to befriend him because their parents wanted to get to know his family. He graduated university and set up his own company as a freelance architect. His family's high-profile connections landed him a lot of work. All of the Marks Hotels built after 2005 were designed by David. His favorite color was blue, he liked his steak rare—she remembered that from their first "date."

She jumped on one foot as she fastened her sandal. *He's a fan of basketball, but not baseball.* She secured a diamanté slide into her hair. *He hates jeans. He doesn't even own a pair.* The doorbell rang and she grabbed her purse, stuffing it with her phone, keys, and wallet. The doorbell rang again, Emily hurried to the door and pressed the button on the intercom.

"Yes, Emily Stewart."

"I think you mean Emily Marks."

Emily sucked in the air through her teeth. The sound of his voice echoing around the apartment sent shivers of excitement running through her veins, a nervous excitement. And she liked it.

"I'll be right down." She ran back to her dresser and picked up the platinum ring, sliding it onto her finger and marveled at it for a moment. She always wondered what it would feel like to wear a beautiful diamond ring and walk around with a man on her arm. Now that it was happening, none of it seemed real. *Which is true, none of it IS real, Emily. Don't forget it.*

She shook her head and hurried out of her apartment, ignoring the twinge of sadness deep within her stomach.

"Wow, you look——" David broke off and held his hand to his heart with a look of admiration. Emily's cheeks warmed and she couldn't stop a beam spreading across her face at his reaction.

"Thanks, you don't look too bad either." She linked her arm with his and traced a line along the cuff of his white shirt. A silver cufflink caught her eye; she leaned closer to study the detail. It was a tiny scroll.

"Mr. and Mrs. Marks, good evening."

Emily jumped at the welcome to see Henry standing beside the limousine as they approached. Emily glanced at David with a knowing smile. She was sure news would spread quickly now that everyone in David's inner circle knew. Emily wondered whether she should tell her family. Isn't this the type of thing you'd tell your sister about? She could offer some advice or talk it through. Emily inwardly scoffed at the thought. *When was the last time she or even my parents called me? They don't care.* Emily brushed away her thoughts and took David's hand as he helped her into the back of the limousine.

"I like your car," she said, pushing herself deeper into the squishy leather seat. David settled into his seat and turned to look at her, matching her expression.

"Thanks. Now, tell me about these investors we are about to meet."

"Honestly, there's not much to tell." Emily shrugged. "Matthew is my contact. I'm not even sure who he is. He's kept the identity of these investors under wraps, so I'm a bit in the dark about them."

"Interesting, and what exactly is your plan?"

"Sorry?"

"What do you need money for?"

Emily clenched her jaw and swallowed. So far, she had made a good show... acted like she didn't have want for anything.

"I want to open up a new office in LA."

"LA?"

"Yes, well it's a hot spot for actors. I think a match-making business will do well there."

"No doubt, that's true. It's a wise business decision."

Emily looked at him with surprise. She had not expected David to have a positive opinion on it.

"Thanks."

"How much are you asking for?"

"Two-hundred and fifty thousand."

"Is that all?"

Well, sure, a quarter of a million dollars is peanuts when you're a billionaire. Emily resisted the urge to huff and roll her eyes. Instead, she pressed her lips together and nodded.

"Why don't you just take out a loan? I'm guessing these people will want a percentage of your business for their investment. Why give it away?"

Emily wanted to pout and fold her arms, insist that it was none of this was his business. Which was true, but did she need to tell him all about her finances? No. But the sincere look in his eye and the gentleness of his voice had Emily's defences lowering.

"Honestly, I'm broke. I'm already up to my eyeballs in debt."

"How is that possible? I've seen your fees. Harold told me you have a whole team with a massive list of clients."

Emily scratched the back of her hand and looked away. She couldn't look into David's eyes for another moment. He didn't get it. Hiring staff with New York expenses, the office alone cost her more than a mortgage payment and then there was getting top interior designers to make the office look trendy. The cost of living, wining and dining potential clients, keeping up with the image of a successful businesswoman. The finances snowballed out of control. But that's why the LA business was going to be a game changer. She was sure she could get higher profile clients, increase profits, and with the help of the investors the slate would be wiped clean and she could start again.

"Is this your first time dealing with investors?"

Emily's stomach tightened. Although his question seemed innocent enough, she sensed that he was questioning her abilities. Had she done anything like this before? No. She looked back at David and remained quiet, listening to the faint rumble of the limousine as they traveled through the city streets. David placed his hand on hers.

"Okay, well I'm happy to help any way I can."

"Have you got two-hundred and fifty thousand dollars lying around?"

David bowed his head as he laughed, then said, "Well...."

"I was joking," Emily added. She looked down at their hands and sat in wonderment of how normal it felt to have David touching her.

"I try not to mix business with pleasure," he said in a low voice. A smile crept across his face as they locked eyes. Emily threw her head back and sighed.

"So, tell me, am I business or pleasure to you?"

David rubbed his chin in thought—one of the gestures she was figuring out about her "husband."

"You mean business," he began, "but being with you is my pleasure."

Emily cocked a brow at him and considered his

response. She wasn't quite sure what he meant, but she had no time to find out because the car came to a stop and David announced, "We're here. Are you ready to schmooze these investors?"

Butterflies fluttered around in her stomach and Emily swallowed nervously.

"Let's do this."

CHAPTER TEN

DINNER AND PLANS

"So, David. Tell me, what do you do?"

David swallowed the last of his drink and placed the glass down on the white table linen; a waiter appeared out of nowhere to top off his glass. David looked up at the large man who addressed him. Mathew was not at all what he pictured. His cheeks were permanently rosy and the veins in his neck were bulging. His Texan slur was the only indication to his hometown. The two men sitting either side of him were quiet and immobile. Their eyes narrowed on him and paid no attention to Emily whatsoever. From the first moment they shook hands, David knew these men wouldn't deal with a woman if they didn't have to. The conversation was solely directed at David after the initial greeting, as if Emily didn't exist. Emily Stewart, the sassy, brilliant, outrageously beautiful business owner, being left in the corner? The thought made David's blood boil; he knew what he needed to do.

"I'm so sorry, will you excuse me for a moment? I need to make a quick call." Without waiting for an answer, David got to his feet and offered Emily an apologetic smile. She nodded at him matter-of-factly and turned to the men across the table.

"So, gentlemen, do any of you use a dating app?"

David strolled across the quiet restaurant and hid behind the large aquarium tank sitting in the center of the room. How long should he give it? Five minutes? Ten? He peered through the murky water and squinted. Emily was flicking her hair back and laughing at something. The men were chuckling back at her.

That's it Emily, just be yourself, they'll love you.

A waiter stopped and asked David if anything was wrong. He waved him off and took his phone out of his pocket to pretend he was making a call. He looked down to see his father's name flash across the screen.

"Father, I can't speak right now, I'm at dinner."

"I need to speak with you."

"It's going to have to wait. I'll be flying into the island in three days, we can talk then."

"No, David, we need to talk now."

David scoffed and glanced up through the fish tank again. Emily's back was straight as a board, and she had her hands resting on the table. She appeared deep in conversation now.

"What is it?"

"Not here, David. I have a car waiting outside the restaurant."

"How do you know where I am?"

"You think you can hide from your father? Now, stop wasting time. This won't take long."

David puffed out the air from his cheeks and strolled out of the restaurant, glancing nervously over his shoulder. Neither the investors nor Emily appeared to notice him leave.

David walked out into the rain and was just about to raise a hand to shield his face, when Joffrey held out an umbrella for him.

"Sorry, sir," he muttered. "You know I've never been able to keep secrets from him." David shot him a look and got into the back of the silver Rolls Royce.

"Evening."

David shook the rain off his jacket and looked at the man sitting with his hands gently clasped together.

"Make this quick, I need to get back inside."

"You don't speak to me like that, David," His father warned. "I'm here to remind you of our arrangement."

David looked down.

"I haven't forgotten."

"Good, because if your grandmother finds out...."

"I'll make sure that doesn't happen."

"Have you spoken to your brother?"

David snorted.

"Have you? Has anyone?"

"He's family, David. And he misses you."

David threw his hands up in exasperation.

"Well, maybe he should stop putting money before family."

"He's a hard worker, you know that."

"At what cost?"

"Please tell me you had her sign a prenup."

David stared at his father, taken aback by the sudden change of topic.

"Of course, Father."

David's father relaxed. "Good. I don't want you to go through what I—"

"You mean when my mother left you and took half of everything."

"It was fortunate your grandmother saw sense enough to keep the shares."

LAURA BURTON

"I know." David sighed and picked at a loose thread in the seam of his trousers.

"You know the terms… your grandmother must approve of your wife before she will amend her will. If you do not want everything to go to your brother, you will do well to prepare Emily."

"I'm not worried. Emily is perfect for—"

"Have you told her?" The words hit David right in the chest, as if shot by a poisonous dart. He shook his head.

"Good, the less she knows about *that*, the better."

David shifted in the seat and rubbed the back of his neck.

"I have to go."

"All right, I'll see you at the island."

David and his father looked at each other silently for a moment before they simultaneously nodded to each other, in mutual understanding.

———

David returned to his seat just as the two men on either side of Mathew stood up.

"Excuse us, we need to fly out to Chicago for an early meeting." They shook hands with David. Emily stood up and reached out her hand.

"Thank you for meeting me," she said as she shook hands with them both.

"We look forward to seeing how this turns out. Mathew will keep us posted."

Mathew offered a salute, and the gentlemen left the restaurant.

"That was fast," David said as he and Emily took their seats. Mathew chortled into his glass.

"Time is money, Mr. Marks. You should know that."

Emily placed her hand on David's, the warmth of her touch sent surprising shivers through him.

"They like my proposal." She gave a dramatic pause, her eyes glinting in the dim lights. "Thankfully, they didn't recognize you, and they're going to invest."

Emily flashed her teeth at him proudly and turned back to Mathew, her hand falling onto her lap as she moved. David's fingers twitched against the burning sensation where her hand touched his skin.

"Great."

Mathew got up from the table and tucked his checked shirt into his pants.

"Well, I'll settle the check." He licked a hand and smoothed down his straw-like hair to the side before straightening his tie.

"You're leaving?" Emily asked.

David couldn't decide if she sounded hopeful or

politely disappointed. Mathew's shoulders shook as he chuckled, the sound bubbled in the back of his throat.

"Like I said, time is money. It was nice to meet you both, and David, next time you're in Texas, give me a shout. I'll show you what a real smokehouse looks like."

David shook his sweaty hand and smiled politely.

"I will," he lied. Mathew swaggered off to the bar walking across the room as if he owned the place. David turned back to Emily.

"They didn't even stay for dessert." Her face paled as she looked at him, most likely in a state of shock knowing the investors were on board.

"Do you want to take dessert back to our place?"

Emily looked pointedly at David with her brows raised. His pulse thumped against his temples as his blood rose to his face by her response.

"I need to get back to *my place*, there's so much to do. I've got calls to make and get things moving before we go to your grandmother's party."

"Which reminds me, if you want to convince my family that you're Mrs. Marks, you will need to look the part."

Emily cocked her head to the side and twirled her hair around her finger. David wanted to run his hands through those curls.

"Oh, what are you thinking?"

He knew she wasn't asking him to tell her what he was literally thinking at that moment. But the truth blurted out of him before he could muster any self-control.

"I can't stop thinking about kissing you."

Emily bit her lip and her cheeks flooded with color at his response. She was irresistible. David swallowed nervously and balled his hands into fists. *Control yourself, David. You're behaving like a teenage boy.* But he couldn't help it. That's just how he felt around Emily. Was he falling for her? So soon?

Emily leaned in and his heart raced. The scent of her floral perfume filled his nostrils and sent his head spinning. He licked his lips and leaned in, anticipating their lips meeting. Instead, Emily brushed her cheek against his and pressed her soft lips against his temple.

"I need to go," she whispered in his ear. David closed his eyes at the sound of her gentle voice. He was under her spell. If she told him to drive off the edge of a cliff, he was certain there would be no hesitation. He nodded.

"All right," he murmured. Emily got to her feet, David grasped her hands and squeezed as he looked up at her.

"Thank you for your help tonight. I couldn't have done this without you," she said softly. David jumped to his feet and looked down at her. The silver clasp in her hair sparkled.

"You could. And you did." He kissed the back of her hand.

"I'll call you," she said, sliding her hands away. She turned and walked confidently out of the restaurant. David looked on, immobile and helpless. He just stood there, forgetting what he was doing, or where he was supposed to go. His father's words echoed in his ears. *The less she knows about that, the better.*

He swallowed the rest of his drink and wiped his mouth with the back of his hand. He wanted to get down on his knees at Emily's feet and confess everything. She was so sure and upfront. He had to tell her.

But would she be able to look at me again, once she knows the truth? He shook his head, determined. He would have to take the risk, she deserved to know. Resolved, he marched out of the restaurant.

CHAPTER ELEVEN

Beautiful Chaos

"Julian, I'm sorry to call so late."

"Everything all right, Emily?" Julian's voice sounded tired echoing out of the phone resting on the table.

"Yes, how are my clients doing?" Emily asked, trying to sound chirpy.

"Can't this wait until tomorrow?"

"You're right, sorry. I wanted to talk to you about the company and the changes—"

"You're opening an office in LA," Julian finished for her in a bored tone.

"How did you know?"

"Everyone knows. It's all you've ever talked about for the last six months."

"Right. Well, it's finally happening."

"Good for you. It's a great move… Why are you calling me?" His frankness set Emily back a bit. She took a breath and frowned.

"I want you to take over the New York office."

Silence.

"Emily… I don't know what to say."

"Say, 'thank you, this is the opportunity of a lifetime,' or something. You've been working alongside me from the beginning, I can't think of anyone more qualified."

"Thank you, Emily, this is the opportunity of a lifetime."

They laughed.

"Really, though, I didn't expect it," he urged.

"I have to go. We'll iron out all the details next week."

"Great, thank you. Enjoy your time off."

Emily ticked off "call Julian" on her check list and sucked on the pen as she looked down the list of items. Then she picked up her phone and placed it on speaker again.

"Hello?"

"Jaqueline, are you sitting down?"

"Ms. Stewart? Yes, yes I am."

"The investors are in. We're moving to LA!"

"Oh, that is great—wait, what?"

"Julian is taking over the New York office, and you are coming with me to LA."

"I'm moving?"

"Yes, of course. You want a promotion, well here it is. I need you to help me set up the new office. Besides, why would you stay in New York?"

"My whole life is here, my family, my boyfriend."

"Jaqueline, there will be plenty of eligible bachelors in LA, I assure you." Emily laughed.

"You're asking me to break up with my boyfriend?" Jaqueline sounded affronted. Like this was not happy news. Emily frowned.

"Are you telling me, you are going to turn down this opportunity to stay with your boyfriend?"

"I want to stay at the New York office."

Emily didn't like the defiant tone of her voice. Jaqueline definitely had more courage when she wasn't face to face with Emily.

"Right. Well, if that's the case you'll have to speak to Julian about that. He might have a job for you in the New York office."

"Julian? Please, no… Ms. Stewart, are you saying that if I don't come with you to LA, I'm fired?"

"No, of course not. I'm saying your job is relocating to LA and if you want to stay in New York, you'll have to apply for a job."

"But—I. Julian doesn't make me feel comfortable."

"It sounds like you have a decision to make, then. I'll let you go and think about it." Emily ended the call before Jaqueline could reply. Moving to LA and getting a promotion was a dream for anyone who'd been working as an assistant for years. Jaqueline was young, inexperienced, and expected Emily to create a perfect career path for her, in the place of her choosing? *What is it with these Millennials?* She pushed the thoughts out of her mind and opened up her laptop.

After forty minutes she was rubbing her temples and yawning, scrolling through the listings. This was going to take a while. She got up from her desk and unzipped her dress, allowing it to fall to her feet. She marched over to the bedroom and pulled on her cotton pants and her favorite sweater. It was the softest item of clothing in her closet and slipped down her right shoulder. Her curls drooped enough to make her hair look more wavy than curly now. She pulled out the clip in her hair and shook her head. The door alarm buzzed, and she stood still, eyes wide and staring at the clock on the wall, before she walked into the living room to hit the buzzer.

"Who is it?"

"Emily, I need to speak to you. Can I come in?"

His voice crackled against the sound of rain pouring over the microphone, but Emily knew who it was. She buzzed him in.

"Come on up." She turned around and eyed her apartment in horror. From the dress lying discarded on the floor, to the stack of papers spread out on the coffee table. She jumped into action, throwing her dress on her bed, collecting empty chocolate wrappers littered around the apartment, and forcefully stacked the dirty dishes in the sink. She swiveled on the spot to the sound of the faint tapping on her door.

"Hi there, long time no see," she said brightly as she pulled the door open. Without her heels on, she had to crane her neck to look up at David's face. His skin was wet and waxy in the yellow light, and a crease along his brow and the firm set to his lips told her he had been thinking too much. He walked into the apartment and started to pace the room.

"Are you okay?" Emily asked warily. She wondered would could possibly have happened in the last handful of hours since she saw him. Perhaps it was something to do with the phone call he had to take at the restaurant? Or maybe he was having second thoughts about their arrangement?

"Hey, do you want to call this off?"

David stopped pacing and stared at her like a rabbit in headlights.

"What?"

Emily closed the door and walked over to him.

"Look, you saw those investors… I don't think they care very much about visiting again. I'm pretty sure we can just go our separate ways."

"That doesn't help *my* situation though, does it?"

Emily grimaced. In all the excitement about planning her move to LA, she forgot about the party with David's family. She owed it to him to follow through.

"I'm sorry," she said hesitantly. "So, if you're not here to call this off? What's wrong?"

David took a deep breath and his eyes floated up and down Emily. She crossed her arms self-consciously and noticed his eyes darkening as he looked at her.

"I need to tell you something."

He averted his eyes and started pacing again. Emily tapped her fingers against her arm waiting. Should she offer him a drink? Maybe take his jacket and hang it up to dry? She wasn't sure what was so important he dragged himself out in the rain.

"You've been nothing but upfront and honest with me since we first met," he said finally. Emily swallowed.

That's not true.

"Listen, I can see this is hard for you… do you want me to take your jacket? You're making the floor wet." She reached out her hands and David stopped moving. He glanced down at the floor and looked at it in shock, as if surprised it even existed. He nodded and handed her the heavy jacket. She eyed the Armani logo on the label before she hung it up.

"There, that's better. Do you want something to drink? Tea, coffee? Hot chocolate?"

"No, I'm all right."

"Why don't you take a seat?" Emily brushed cookie crumbs off the couch and motioned for him to sit; they sat side by side, staring at each other.

"I like you too."

Emily started and blinked several times.

Is this what's eating him up inside? Her shoulders relaxed.

"Is that it? Goodness David… the way you were acting. I thought you were going to tell me you murdered someone and needed help hiding the body."

David chuckled to himself with the faintest smile. Emily caught sight of something flash behind his eyes. She couldn't help but wonder if he had more to say. David cleared his throat and clasped his hands together.

"I'm sorry to show up so late, I was just thinking…."

"Yes?" Emily leaned down to look into his eyes as she placed a hand on his knee. He flinched against her touch.

Why did he do that? Emily had replayed their kiss

on repeat in her mind, it kept her awake at night. And they had been shamelessly flirting all afternoon. *Now he's flinching at my touch?* She eyed the hollow of his neck and suppressed the urge to trace her fingers along his collarbone. David turned his head and looked at her, he placed a hand on top of hers and his lips curved upward. Emily forgot what they were talking about. Sitting this close to his face, that beautiful masculine jaw, and those tender lips… her breaths became shallow and uneven as a hunger grew within the pit of her stomach.

"I do think we should be living together." His low grunt sent flurries of excitement through Emily's midriff.

"Don't you think that's a bit soon?" Their faces were less than a foot apart, and she could sense the heat rising off his cheeks.

"People will wonder why you keep coming back here." He looked around, a twinge of disdain washed over his face before he corrected himself with a casual smirk. Emily frowned and crossed her arms.

"Do you know how expensive it is to have an apartment in the city… for normal people."

"Oh, and you're normal?" David laughed.

"I'm not a bazillionaire!"

"A what?" They both threw their heads back and chuckled. "That sounds like a dinosaur."

Emily loosened her arms and rested her hands in her lap. David leaned in close and brushed her cheek with his knuckles. "And anyway, you are not normal, Mrs. Marks."

Emily inhaled deeply, taking in his scent. Once again, her brain emptied all thought or memory of their conversation and she became lost in the moment. Her instincts woke up like a sleeping lion, starving. She licked her bottom lip, his eyes darted down showing her he noticed. She gulped. Their chemistry was electrifying, and Emily was sure that if someone were to walk in, they would see strobes of light ricocheting off the walls. What was David doing in her apartment? Why did she think she could act serious, sitting on her crumb-infested couch, wearing a sweater with a giant bunny on the front? This was so far from the respectable businesswoman exterior she liked to put on. David was still wearing a suit, but the top two buttons of his grey shirt were undone and his hair was tousled in waves around his ears. Emily wondered if he grew it out, would his head be covered in curls? David turned to her as if to say something but he remained silent.

"Why am I not normal?" she asked as she gave him a nudge. David tugged at his collar, a flush of color rising up his neck. *Is he nervous? Why are you so shy now, Mr. Marks?* She leaned in to kiss him, the luring scent of his cologne and the faint blush over his cheeks were too much to resist. She wanted to place her hands *every-where* and kiss him until morning. David stood up as Emily froze, leaning awkwardly to the space David had been. She tilted her head to the side to look up at him, a giant in her living room.

"I should go."

"But you just asked me to live with you?"

"Right," he said, slightly breathless. "*We* should go. Do you need help packing your bags?"

"Excuse me? You think I'm just going to come along and play house in your fancy top-floor apartment?"

"It has three bedrooms; you'll have your own space... I'll make sure you're comfortable."

Emily slowly rose to her feet and folded her arms as she looked at him with the most self-respecting, serious pout she could muster.

"Oh really?" She surveyed his face. There it was again, a flash of something behind his eyes. *What is going on in that gorgeous head of yours?*

David walked over to the kitchen area and opened the cupboards, looking for something. He found two mugs and pulled them out and set them on the counter. Emily watched him open the refrigerator.

"What are you doing?"

David's head popped up past the breakfast bar and he puffed out the air in his cheeks.

"Do you have any milk?"

"No, I'm dairy-free."

"Got any dairy-free milk?"

"David, what are you doing?" Emily repeated, this time her bafflement turned into irritation. He was behaving oddly. She couldn't work out why.

David's shoulders slumped and he kicked the refrigerator door closed with his foot.

"You know what, because you're doing me a massive favor, I'm going to buy you a whole new wardrobe tomorrow. Just come as you are." He eyed her up and down and Emily tucked her hair behind her ear.

"Are you sure? You really want me to move in?"

"Well, just for now, at least. Until my grandmother…." He didn't finish the sentence. But he didn't need to. Until she died. So that was his plan? *Is this his conscience kicking in?* Lying to your terminally ill grandmother just to get your inheritance seemed pretty low. Yes, Emily lied too, but that was different. That was to pacify obnoxious, narrow-minded investors who thought it was the 1950s and a woman couldn't run a successful matchmaking business without being married. Totally different. Emily rested her hands on her hips and looked down at her outfit.

"I'll have to change…."

"Don't."

Emily's head snapped back up and she looked at David who was staring at her with dark eyes. A smile etched on his face and her cheeks heated under his gaze.

"No, I'm going to change out of this ridiculous—"

"I like it," his words were firm and final. Emily closed her mouth and sighed. Then she shrugged.

"You have a car, I presume?" She arched her back and glanced out of the window at the streets below, but the window pane was black and she couldn't see anything. She imagined Henry sitting in the limousine listening to classical music.

"We're a couple of hours into the weekend now," David said as he took a step forward. Whatever traces of regret plagued his mind, were clearly long-forgotten. He took another step; he was standing so close now, Emily had to lean back to see his face. She automatically raised her hands to his arms and grasped his biceps. They flexed under her touch. There it was again, the chemistry swirling around them, emitting bolts of electricity in different parts of her body. Emily's mouth became dry as she swallowed. She was thirsty, but it was the sort of thirst that couldn't be satisfied with a drink.

"We have a lot to do to get ready. I need to warn you my family are… intense." David's voice vibrated in Emily's ears. She smiled drunkenly at him.

"I can handle myself."

David cupped her face in his soft hands.

I wonder if he uses moisturizer. Billionaire moisturizer, probably.

"I know you can." David lowered his face and Emily did her best impression of a sexy pout. Anticipating the kiss, her toes curled, and she clutched his arms, pulling him in closer. They were less than a hairsbreadth apart when the phone rang. Emily and David froze, their eyes locked onto each other. Neither of them moved for a few moments, in a strange standoff as the cheerful ringtone sounded. The moment fizzled away and the two of them stepped back, David pulled out his phone from his pants.

"Sorry," he murmured. Emily twirled her hair with her fingers and eyed the clock on the wall.

"Who's calling you at this hour?"

"Henry, are you all right?"

Emily crossed the room and squinted through the window with her hand to her brow. She could just make out the car.

"Yes, everything is fine, we'll be down in a minute."

Emily turned to look at David who clapped his hands.

"Come on, let's take you to your new home."

CHAPTER TWELVE

ULTERIOR MOTIVES

David stretched out on his back and stared up at the bedroom ceiling of his penthouse. He couldn't sleep. Not with his imagination running wild, knowing that Emily was sleeping in the room across the hall. Or was she lying awake too? He rolled onto his side and propped himself up on an elbow, patting the empty space next to him. He balled his hand into a fist and sunk his head low with regret. He couldn't do it. He couldn't tell her the truth. The sight of her standing in her apartment, her hair a beautiful mess, wearing the most adorable pink pants and white sweater with the cartoon bunny on the front.

She looked ten times more attractive dressed in comfortable clothes, than in her business dresses. She stared at him with such vulnerability, he lost all motivation to confess. How could he? Her face was flushed and he noticed excitement in her eyes. Her dreams were coming true. It was only a matter of time before his grandmother finally succumbed to the cancer in her frail body, and the legalities would be sorted out. He wondered how his motivations appeared to Emily. Did she think he was shallow? That he was just in this for the money? The truth was, he didn't care about the money. He cared about doing what was right. And he made a promise to his father. He gritted his teeth as his mind replayed a conversation they shared a few weeks ago.

"*Her name is Emily Stewart,*" *Charles said, handing over a file to David.* "*She is key to this plan.*" *David looked down at the picture of the most beautiful woman he had ever seen. Her confident smile, enchanting eyes framed with long black lashes and a cascade of dark hair flowing over one shoulder had him staring with his mouth open. He looked up at Charles.*

"*What is the plan, exactly?*"

Charles cleared his throat and swirled the drink in his hand. "*You need to marry her, before your grandmother passes, and you* better do it soon. *The doctors inform me that we may only have weeks.*"

"*Who is she? How did you find out about her?*" David's mouth turned dry as he glanced at the photograph again.

"*You remember Harold? She set him up with his wife.*"

"*How am I going to get a stranger to fall in love with me so quickly? I've never even had a girlfriend.*"

"*This isn't about love, David. This is about saving the family business.*"

David stood and walked across the room as he rubbed the back of his neck. "*I don't like this. Why should we drag anyone else into our family politics?*"

Charles joined him near the window and placed a hand on his shoulder. "*This is how we survive.*"

"*What am I supposed to do? How do I get her to marry me so fast?*"

Charles straightened and looked out of the window. "*Tell her you have to find a wife in thirty days… that'll get her attention. Then play along. Go on a few dates.*"

"*How is that going to help?*"

Charles turned to look steely at David. "*Just stick with the plan and leave the rest to me.*"

. . .

David rolled onto his back and shut his eyes. The conversation still ringing in his ears. He should have told her the truth. *But she is so happy.* Now, she was in his penthouse suite... right where he needed her. David opened his eyes and stretched his arm over the empty side of the bed. *No, she's not where I need her.* His heart raced at the thought. Was this what it was like to fall for someone? He had been so sheltered and protected all his life, then thrown into his work, that he never got the opportunity to meet someone. Anyone. Even making friends was difficult. Now, for the first time in his life, his marital status required his full attention. He just never expected it to turn out like this. Amongst the web of lies lay something warm and authentic. Like a beating heart. Emily looked so casual, with her usually tamed hair frizzing at the ends, her make-up smudged under her eyes... and that outfit. David swallowed, then grinned so wide he felt it in his eyebrows. *She is adorable.* He wanted to wrap his arms around her and hold her. Kiss her. Confess everything. He sensed she had feelings too. But could he bring himself to go there while he hid the truth from her? No. Their initial meeting was built on a bed of lies. He didn't want a relationship to develop, only for her to wonder if any of it was real.

Maybe he could have it all? Emily was perfect. *Of*

course, she's perfect. His father scouted her out for him. David wrestled with his thoughts, biting down on his knuckles with frustration. He thought about marching across the hall, barging into Emily's room, getting down on his knees, and telling her everything. Begging for her forgiveness. Declare his true feelings and… and what? He scoffed. Wake her up, invade her privacy, force her to forgive him. Not a good plan.

But maybe when the truth was out, the whole truth, along with his intense desire to make this relationship real… Maybe they could have it all? With that hopeful thought, David's body finally relaxed, allowing him to sink into a dreamless sleep.

David pressed the palms of his hands against the marble tile and closed his eyes, allowing the muscles in his back to loosen against the warm spray of the shower. He inhaled, filling the lungs with menthol steam and turned the faucet. The heat faded and cold splashes drenched his body, extinguishing the intense passion that had woken him up.

Gritting his teeth, he stepped out of the shower and dried off. His brain wrestled with the thought of telling Emily about his father's agreement, and how he'd heard of her. But not only that—more than anything—he wanted to admit the awkward truth, so he could tell her what he really wanted her to know. *That my feelings are real. I need her.*

David pulled on a pair of dark pants and flung a towel over his right shoulder. His ruffled his damp hair and brushed his teeth, all the while trying not to guess what Emily was doing at that moment. Every time his brain settled on thoughts of her, the heat and tension in his body rose.

"Omeba, schedule an emergency appointment with Noelle."

"Sending Noelle Sunderland a message now. Is there anything else I can help you with?"

"Tell the kitchen to prepare breakfast."

"Yes, Mr. Marks."

Jitters ran up and down David's body and he threw himself on the floor into a plank pose. He huffed and puffed as he did a handful of push ups and stood again, his heart rate thumped against his eardrums and his arms tingled. He only had a couple of hours of actual sleep, but he was buzzing with adrenaline.

After the quick fifteen-minute power workout, he strode across his room and pulled on a blue polo shirt. Taking a deep breath, he took a moment to compose himself, his hand hovering over the silver handle of his bedroom door. Then he pushed it open and walked out into the living area. The sunlight streamed through the large pane windows and cast a dreamy glow over the furniture in the room. His eyes darted around, searching for her. And there she was.

Emily sat hunched over the breakfast bar, her long dark hair was damp and left wet patches down the back of her cotton shirt. She was chewing her bottom lip while reading her phone. The sight of her sent David's senses running wild again. He wondered how many cold showers were in his future.

He needed to tell her the truth, because he *needed her*.

CHAPTER THIRTEEN

A Billionaire Makeover

E mily looked up from her phone to see David standing across the room staring at her. His arms were bulging and his wet hair glistened.

"Morning." She tucked her hair behind an ear. "You don't have a hairdryer do you? I forgot to pack mine." She tried to towel dry her hair the best she could without making it frizz, but without a dryer she knew she was fighting a losing battle.

David didn't speak for a moment. Or move. Emily raised her brows and wondered whether he was in shock. Perhaps he had forgotten that she stayed over? Emily wasn't sure. But something stopped him in his tracks and the look in his eyes was difficult to read. She jumped down from the high stool and placed her phone on the counter top.

"Are you okay?"

She walked barefoot across the floor, closing the space between them a little more with every step. Once she was close enough to see his pupils, he jumped into action.

"Morning, sorry. I think I'm still half asleep."

His face transformed from a look of shock to a casual smile. He took a couple of steps forward and bent down to kiss Emily on the cheek. She touched his arm and turned her face to meet his lips but before they touched, David jumped back like he'd been electrocuted.

"What's wrong?"

"Nothing, everything is… I'm mean you're… look at you."

Emily's eyes narrowed. She watched David awkwardly lean against the couch, stumbling as he slipped and swinging his arms to catch his balance. *Is he nervous?*

"You're being weird," she said frankly as she crossed her arms. David's cheeks grew pink.

"If I'm honest, I've never had a woman… here."

"I was here the other night. You didn't seem so shy, then."

David's whole face was crimson now. Emily wasn't sure whether the sight was adorable or irritating. Why wouldn't he kiss her? She glanced at the couch and her mind replayed their kiss from the other night. He seemed so sure, confident, *sexy*. Now, he was floundering and appeared to have no idea what to do with his hands.

"Having you here is… big for me."

"You asked me to come, though. I can leave if it makes you feel more comfortable."

"No," David said quickly. Perhaps a little too quickly for his own liking because a faint look of horror crossed his face. Then he smiled in a feign attempt to look cool and austere.

"I know you said you haven't had a girlfriend before… but you've—you know—had women…."

"Oh sure." David was nodding with a knowing frown. "Loads."

"Loads?" Emily suppressed the urge to laugh.

"Hundreds."

David squared his shoulders. Emily raised a hand to her mouth.

"David Marks, you are a terrible liar."

David's shoulders slumped and he exhaled. The act was over. *Wow, he couldn't keep that up for long. Just how does he think he can pretend to be married and convince his family?*

"Never."

The word hit Emily somewhere in her midriff and stirred a flurry of excitement. His sincere gaze told her he was being honest. She gently took his hand.

"No one? At your age?"

"I just never found…."

Emily rolled her eyes.

"Don't tell me, 'the one'?" Emily studied David's face. He just nodded intently. She squeezed his hand, her heart melting.

"Well, I don't know what to say about that." She took a breath. "But If we are going to pull this off, you're going to have to get comfortable with me fast."

"What did you have in mind?" David's posture relaxed; Emily could see him returning to his normal self again. Talking to him seemed to be helping. "Well you can start"—she took his hand and placed it on the small of her back—"by getting used to touching me like I'm your wife, rather than an electric fence." David's lips curved upwards. She gently tugged on his shirt, pulling him in close. She could see dark rings underneath his eyes and wondered if he had slept at all. *That would explain his odd behavior*, she mused.

Emily reached up and interlocked her fingers behind his neck, standing on tip-toes. David lowered to meet her and the two of them stared at each other lovingly. Emily caught sight of him licking his lips; she had butterflies in her stomach.

"I can't resist you," David whispered to her.

"Then don't," Emily whispered back. She leaned forward to meet his lips when a knock on the door had them break apart in a flash.

"Yes," David wheezed. He coughed like he had the air knocked out of him. The door opened and a short man wearing a perfectly pressed suit entered pushing a food cart.

"Your breakfast, sir, ma'am."

Emily was startled at being addressed. She nodded to him and watched David stroll over and clap his hand on the man's back.

"Thank you, Jonathan. It is Jonathan, right?"

The man stared up at him and a look of sheer delight flooded his face.

"Yes, sir, you're welcome. Is there anything else I can do for you?" Jonathan clasped his hands together.

"Could you have someone bring up a hair dryer?" David glanced at Emily. She grinned sheepishly and pointed to her hair. The man gave a crisp nod, then vacated the room. Once the door was closed David turned back to Emily. He scratched his neck sheepishly, perhaps considering whether to invite her to sit down and eat or throw her onto the couch and satisfy other appetites. For Emily, however, the moment was gone. The brief interruption reminded her to keep focused on the task. This was a temporary situation; soon enough, David's grandmother will have passed away, the shares would be in his name and Emily would be free to move to LA and start her new life. Was it fair to lead him on and think this plan would turn out any differently? Did she want it to be any different? Emily realized she was staring into space and blinked as she brought herself back, then looked at David, who appeared to be lost in his own thoughts

"What's for breakfast?" Emily asked, David met her gaze, then shook his head and clapped.

"Right, breakfast." He lifted the metal lids of the plates.

"Oh, how did you know I love croissants?" Emily said in a revered tone as she reached out to pick up the French pastry. The warm bread scent wafted over Emily's nostrils and her stomach rumbled in response.

"I'm starving." Her focus was now completely on eating. Emily loved food. She thought that perhaps, she loved food more than people. She caught sight of David standing immobile in her peripheral vision, she swallowed and looked at him.

"Are you not going to eat?"

David poured a glass of orange juice and lifted the glass to his lips. "I'm not sure I'm feeling hungry." He gulped down the entire drink.

Emily picked up a clementine and mindlessly peeled it as she watched David take a seat at the table.

As she went to take a seat next to him, a knock at the door stopped her in her tracks.

"Shall I get that?" she whispered. David waved a hand aside.

"Come in."

The door swung open and Emily jumped back in surprise. A huge curtain rail moved into the room, dresses swung side to side with the movement, and someone mumbled from behind the rail.

"Hello?" Emily peered around the clothes to see a very thin woman, wearing horn-rimmed glasses and an entirely black pant suit. Her auburn, straw-like hair was cut so severely around her face, it looked to Emily like a badly-made wig.

The lady peered at Emily over her glasses and pursed her lips. "I can see why you called."

A chair scraped across the floor and the sound echoed around the room. Emily snapped her head back to see David dabbing his mouth with a napkin as he marched over to the woman.

"Noelle, thank you for coming so fast." He kissed her cheek and her thin lips curved upward as she closed her eyes.

"Of course, David. When I heard you got married, I knew exactly what you needed me to do." Noelle held out a hand to Emily, she took it and tried to suppress the urge to frown at her.

"Emily Stewart, nice to meet—" Emily cut her words short at the sight of the woman's expression. She glanced over at David who looked at her pointedly. "Sorry, Emily Marks, I'm still getting used to that." She shook Noelle's hand confidently and covered her mistake with a laugh. Emily didn't realize they were telling *everyone* that they were married. She needed to think fast on her feet.

"Nice to meet you, Emily, I'm Noelle, an old friend of David's." She patted David's cheek with a wrinkly hand, her nails were painted black and had a dazzling shine to them. Emily forced a smile.

"I'm here to make you look good."

"I think I can take care of myself," Emily stated. But Noelle tutted and marched to her clothes rail, disregarding her as she spoke to David.

"Your PA sent across the details of your grand-mother's party," Noelle said as she stood up straight and held out three dresses to Emily. She raised each one out and squinted before tossing them aside.

"No, no, no this will not do," she muttered as she dove back into the endless supply of clothes. Emily pick up one of the discarded dresses that still had a price tag on it, which was more than her credit card balances combined.

"I can leave you both to it. I should make some

calls anyway." David started to walk away, but Emily grabbed his arm and stared at him with pleading eyes.

"Don't leave me with her," she whispered.

David patted her hand gently. "It'll be fine. Let her work her magic. She'll make you look great, don't worry."

That wasn't what Emily was worried about. She stared helplessly at David as he strode out of the room and disappeared behind a door. Noelle reappeared again with a bundle of new dresses, probably weighing more than the woman herself.

"Don't worry, you're in good hands."

CHAPTER FOURTEEN

First Class Feelings

After making some important calls for work, David fell into an exhausted heap on his bed and slept the rest of the morning away. Orange sunlight flooded his room and he basked in its golden rays. He stretched his arms and yawned loudly. A babble of voices pricked his ears up and he marched over to his bedroom door. He re-entered the lounge area and his jaw dropped to the floor.

Emily stood up on a stool wearing a knee-length wraparound dress. The nude material sat snug on her form and gathered at her left hip. David's eyes followed the line of the dress up to the plain bodice and looked up at Emily's face. Her eyes lingered on him and she gave him a wry smile. Noelle was circling Emily unintelligibly muttering to herself—one of her many quirky traits. She was the family dressmaker and designer for as long as he could remember. How she kept her job working for the Marks family, David had no idea. It must have had something to do with the fact that she was brilliant.

David walked over to them and applauded slowly, still staring at Emily in wonderment.

"You look...."

"Like your wife, yes, David. That was the idea." She interjected, grinning at him with her hands on her hips. Her tanned arms were enhanced by the nude shade of her dress. And her long hair was swept up into a loose knot at the back of her head. Strays of flyaway hairs softened her face and her plump lips sported a fresh layer of rose lipstick. She was staring at him with a confident smile. Her sassy attitude was back, and David loved it. He wanted to collapse to his knees and declare his feelings, but Noelle was hovering around like a bad smell.

"Did you find everything you need?"

"Of course, she did," Noelle snapped before Emily could reply. David opened his mouth, but Noelle wasn't finished speaking. "She has enough to keep her going for now, but I'll be back with a collection tomorrow. Her neck looks rather bare." She gave him a pointed look. "You would do you well to pay Oliver a visit."

David nodded and muttered his thanks. And like that, Noelle collected her belongings and pushed the clothes rail out of the room. Emily stepped down from the stool and spun around on the spot.

"What do you think of my new dress?"

"What do *you* think of it? That's all that matters."

Emily frowned at him. "Actually, you're paying for it, so I think your opinion matters."

"I'm happy if you're happy," he said, trying to be diplomatic. He couldn't think of anything to say. Would it be too creepy to admit he found her the sexiest woman alive in that dress? Or that it was the perfect blend between professional and drop-dead-gorgeous? Even in his thoughts, that sounded weird.

"I'm happy." Emily twirled again and swaggered her hips as she crossed the room to grab a drink.

"For what it's worth, I think you look amazing," David said, finding his courage again. His heart pounded in his chest and his ears were ringing. Emily shook her head to herself as she took a sip of her drink.

"See? Was that really so hard?" She glanced at her phone on the breakfast bar; it vibrated loudly against the granite and she reached out for it. David thought she was going to take the call, but instead she rolled her eyes and put it down again.

"Don't you need to get that?"

Emily took another sip of her drink. "No, it's just my sister," she said after she swallowed.

"Ah, you have a sister. Does she live in New York too?"

David thought there was a mild look of irritation flash across her face but she seemed to recover herself before she smiled politely at him.

"Yes, but we don't see each other."

"Why am I sensing there's a story there?"

"Because there is. And it's a long one."

"Well." David grabbed his jacket from the coat stand and picked up his keys off the small table by the door. "Why don't you tell me all about it while we go."

"Go where?" Emily asked, her arms folded. David smirked at her.

"To see my friend Oliver."

The dark limousine pulled up outside a sky rise building. David got out and held the door open for Emily and held her hand as she stepped onto the sidewalk. When she stood up and looked around, her neck curved slightly and she had baby hairs scattered along her neckline. The space between her hairline and the material of her dress was just wide enough for David to slip his hand there. His fingers twitched against the urge to grab her neck and swoop her in his arms. Emily smiled at him, looking blissfully unaware of David's thoughts. *Does she really not understand how irresistible she is?* He swallowed against the dryness in his mouth and cleared his throat. Henry passed him a bottle of water.

"Here, sir," he said in a low voice. David took an appreciative gulp and looked around. Another car pulled up and the back door swung open. Joffrey and Robert climbed out and stood uniformly beside him. He nodded in acknowledgement.

"Shall we go?"

"Go where? We're in a back alley," Emily said through a laugh. David enjoyed watching her reactions and wondered what other things he could arrange just so he could watch Emily's response.

"We don't go in through the front entrance, too much attention. Besides, the back of the store is where the really good stuff is."

Emily's brow raised at him and she cocked her head to the side. He imagined placing his hand against her cheek and caressing her ear with his thumb. *Snap out of it.*

The group of them walked to the steel door in the

back of the building and David tapped on it. The door clicked and swung open, revealing an elderly man wearing a silver-grey suit.

"David, this is a nice surprise," he said mildly as he stepped back and David walked in. Oliver was an old friend of his father's and had been providing jewelry for the Marks family for decades. He wouldn't ever think to go to anyone else.

"Oliver, I would like to introduce you to my wife." The words sent a flurry of excitement within his stomach. *My wife. I like the sound of that.*

As David walked further into the building, he stopped at a dark room, lined with glass cabinets with dim spotlights showcasing the contents. He heard Emily and Oliver exchange greetings and turned to see them shaking hands. Emily was so poised, refined as she pressed her lips together and held her hand out with confidence. Even in the dim light, her eyes shone.

"It is charming to meet you, Mrs. Marks. May I call you Emily?" Oliver said holding her hand with both of his.

Emily inclined her head. "Of course." Her voice was light and rich, like a songbird, but David knew this was just one facet of her personality. His mind took him back to the night in her apartment. *The real Emily has long wavy hair and wears bunny pjs.* No, Emily wasn't just a girl who loved to let her hair down and wear pjs.

She was everything. Passionate and driven, quick-witted and ambitious. She could hold herself and carry her end of the conversation. Not intimidated by anyone, yet gentle as well.

"So what can I help you both with?" He noticed Oliver struggling to take his eyes off Emily.

I know the feeling.

"My grandmother's birthday is coming up, and we are going to the island to celebrate with her. It's the first time my family will be meeting Emily, and I would like to really make her shine. If you know what I mean."

Oliver beamed at Emily, the admiration in his eyes was obvious as he squeezed her hands, with no apparent intention of letting them go.

"You, my dear, already shine," he said gentlemanly. Emily's cheeks flushed with color as she glanced at David. He wasn't sure if she was loving the attention or planning her escape. There was something behind her eyes that made him think she was not entirely comfortable.

"Nevertheless, I have just the collection for you," Oliver continued, finally allowing Emily's hands to drop and he walked across the room. He motioned for Emily to follow.

She glided toward the cabinet and followed Oliver with her hands clasped behind her back. David's eyes lowered and he stared at the nude open-toe shoes with a six-inch heel. He wondered how she could walk so easily while practically standing on tip-toes.

A vibration in his pocket snapped him out of his thoughts and he pulled out his phone.

"I just need to take this call, excuse me."

"You go ahead, we'll be fine."

David caught sight of Emily staring at him with panicked eyes before she blinked and offered a gracious smile to Oliver.

"You can have whatever you want, darling." He walked up and touched her arm briefly in reassurance. Her face had drained of color. He didn't have time to think on it, though, as he put the phone to his ear and left the room.

"Father."

"David. It's your grandmother."

CHAPTER FIFTEEN

EXPENSIVE TASTES

Emily stiffened as Oliver fastened the clasp of the necklace and it rested like an iron chain on her collarbone. Oliver held out a mirror and eyed her with anticipation.

"There, what do you think?" His voice was low and reverent. Emily stared at the yellow gemstones the size of grapes linked together in a chain.

"It is very pretty," Emily offered, her voice was a little too high to be convincing. The weight of the necklace along with the darkness of the room had her feeling claustrophobic. She wanted to tear it off and run out into the street.

"They are sapphire gemstones and the metal is twenty-four karat gold." An assistant entered the room and Oliver nodded to him.

"Do you have anything... more subtle?" Emily asked as she chewed her lip. Twenty-four karat gold? Sapphires? She dared not ask how much it was, and there was no price tag. *Of course, there's no price tag.* Emily was no stranger to expensive clothes and jewelry. But this was on an entirely different level.

Oliver surveyed her for a moment, then motioned for his assistant. The young man sped to his side and leaned in for Oliver to whisper something into his ear. Emily watched on curiously and swayed side to side slightly on her heels. Noelle had given her the most unpractical pair of shoes and insisted she wear them. She longed to kick them off and walk around barefoot, though she would never do that in public.

"Here, let's see how this does?" Oliver unfastened the sapphire necklace and handed it to his assistant, who gingerly held it in his nimble hands. Oliver turned and held out a delicate string of white and yellow diamonds. Emily admired the way it sparkled in the spotlights.

"They look like sunflowers," she said barely above a whisper. Oliver nodded.

"Yes, that is because they are sunflowers," he said as he fastened the back. He stood away and held up the mirror. Emily touched the necklace lightly and stared at the mirror in wonderment.

"It's beautiful," she said, mostly to herself. The necklace was light, and a string of sunflowers danced across her collarbone.

"How much?" she asked. Thinking she would buy it herself. David had already paid for her clothes. She didn't feel comfortable letting him buy her expensive jewelry too.

"For you, Mrs. Marks, I wouldn't accept anything more than the cost price." The skin around Oliver's eyes creased as he smiled at Emily with his hands pressed together. "Three hundred thousand."

Emily resisted the urge laugh. Three hundred thousand dollars? Suddenly, the necklace weighed heavy on her chest as anxiety flooded her veins. *Act natural. You're a billionaire housewife, remember? That's like pocket change for the Marks family.* She couldn't stand the thought of having David pay for this necklace. The price tag was the same as her mortgage. There was no way she could raise enough money. How could she keep up the act that she was David's wife and get out of the jewelers without the necklace?

Emily did not have to worry, because the door flung open and David charged in. His brows heavy set and his face in a brooding expression.

"Sorry, Oliver, we need to leave." He nodded to

Joffrey and Robert who walked out of the room. Emily's hands shot up to the necklace and she fumbled with the clasp.

"I hope everything is okay?" Oliver asked mildly as he carefully took the necklace from her hands.

Emily didn't wait another moment. This was her opportunity to get out of there. "Thank you for your help. I'm sorry we couldn't stay longer," she said politely and made for the door. David stayed behind.

"Can I see that?" she heard him say to Oliver just before the door swung shut.

Having come from a dark room, the sunlight was blinding and Emily squinted to allow her eyes to adjust. The busy rush of the New York traffic flooded her ears and she basked in the sound for a few moments, taking a deep breath of taxi fumes in the air.

"Mrs. Marks." Emily's eyes snapped open and she blinked looking for the owner of the voice. Robert was standing in front of her and shifted to the side to block the sunshine from hitting her eyes.

"Please, will you call me Emily," she said exasperated. The bodyguards knew this was a charade. They didn't need to make her feel any more uncomfortable. Robert inclined his head.

"As you wish. Mr. Marks has asked me to take you to the car." Emily nodded to him and followed him into the limousine idling a few feet away. As she lowered herself into the car, she caught sight of David approaching, hot on his heels.

"Everything okay?" she asked, once they were both seated and the car door closed.

"I need you to do me another favor." David's look was severe. His eyes bore into hers and sent flurries of excitement through her.

"What is it?" she asked, wondering what he could possibly need from her.

"Henry, take us to the registry office. Robert should have given you the address."

Henry nodded and a small divider raised to the ceiling and hid the front of the car from view. David turned back to Emily, she cocked a brow at him.

"I need you to marry me. Today."

Emily's mouth fell open.

CHAPTER SIXTEEN

BIG PROMISES

David's heart was racing. He stared into Emily's dark eyes and searched for a sign. He wasn't sure what kind of sign he was looking for, exactly. Happiness? Excitement? Fear? Emily's expressive face was a mixture between forlorn and sympathy. Not exactly the response he was hoping for. But time had run out. If they didn't do this quick, everything would be in vain.

David took a breath and told Emily the news. His grandmother had taken a bad turn and was requesting for everyone to come. Her anticipated birthday party was going to take place as soon as the guests arrived.

That wasn't all. David's father explained that his grandmother's lawyer would require evidence of David's marriage to Emily. Faking a relationship wasn't enough.

Emily graciously agreed. David clenched his jaw and silently berated himself. This was not going the way he planned. Now that he had developed feelings for Emily, he wanted to make things right. Tell her the truth, the whole truth, and nothing but the truth. He wanted to have an honest relationship with her. They were on the way to the justice of the peace to get married, and there was no time to explain why he needed the share in the family business. How he'd known of her. The promise he made to his father. All of it. And yet he told her nothing. Even on the car ride to the office, his brain buzzing with thoughts and his heart pounding in his chest. He could have grabbed her hands and told her everything there and then. And pray that she found it in her heart to forgive him, to understand his situation and to go ahead with the nuptials. But the risks were too high. She'd need time to think about it. To process all that information—but they didn't have time.

The car pulled to a stop and Henry opened the door for them.

"I can't believe this is happening." Emily said, her

voice wavering. David grasped her hand and squeezed it tight.

"Thank you so much for doing this." He looked at her, the loose knot on the back of her head was falling out and bobbed up and down with her steps. Her face had paled, and she squeezed his hand back.

"This is crazy, you know that, right?"

David nodded; his mouth was suddenly dry. Emily gave him a pointed stared, proceeded push open the doors to the justice of the peace.

"Okay, as long as we both agree."

"You may now kiss the bride."

David was feeling jittery as he leaned down and softly pressed his lips onto Emily's. Even though the situation was forced and under a stressful time restraint, the action of kissing Emily felt like the most natural thing in the world. As if David was born to kiss her. And only her. For the rest of his life.

"Congratulations, Mr. and Mrs. Marks." David and Emily broke apart and he looked at the tiny woman who'd married them, then he turned his heard to the sound of clapping. Henry, Robert, and Joffrey were the only other people in the room. He caught sight of the mild disapproval in Joffrey's eyes but ignored it. He knew he'd been reckless. Legally, Emily was his wife and they had not signed a prenup; he was now exposed and vulnerable.

But there wasn't any time to dwell on the situation. David took Emily by the hand and lead them out into the streets of New York.

"Time to meet your new family."

CHAPTER SEVENTEEN

Confessions

I just married David. I just married David. I just married *David!*

No matter how many times she thought it in her head, she couldn't comprehend it. Had she just made a mammoth mistake? All sense of reason escaped her as they hurried down the steps, and she bit her tongue to stop from laughing as they got into the car.

Emily was not raised in a loving family. Affection and words of appreciation were rare to find—even from her own parents. It made Emily cautious of trusting people and opening up her feelings. But when she looked at David, her heart warmed. He was gentle, and kind. He made her feel… everything. It was like she found an old friend from a forgotten past. *Maybe soul mates are real?*

"Well, it's going to be a lot easier to tell people I'm your wife now," Emily said brightly, pulling herself out of her thoughts. She rubbed the side of her pinky across the engagement ring on her wedding finger and eyed David carefully. He appeared to be having an internal battle. A slight smile flashed across his face before setting into a serious brooding expression.

"Hey," she said as she placed her hand on his knee. David looked at her. "I did this willingly."

David's expression relaxed and he nodded.

"I'm just sorry we had to go this far... it makes things a lot more complicated."

Emily looked out of the window and nodded in thought. Just over two weeks ago, they were perfect strangers when David came in to find a wife. Emily sabotaged that plan and ended up becoming his wife. She bit her lip against the grin invading her frown.

It didn't seem all that complicated to her. Yet, she supposed it should. The investors were onboard, there was no need for her to officially get married. But she did, happily. She was doing that to help David with his situation. But this was more than doing David a favor now. She was truly happy.

I married David and I'm happy about it.

The thought made her giddy inside.

Emily looked at his tormented expression and her smile faltered. She guessed he was feeling guilty about dragging her into this. But he didn't know the lengths she went to ensure he did. She needed him to stop looking at her like she was the victim. He deserved to know the truth. She bit her lip and looked out of the window.

As the car swung round the corner and they neared their destination, Emily turned back to David, resolved. She was going to tell him the truth. Without wasting another moment.

"David, I have a confession to make," she said in a low murmur. David's eyes widened. As if he never expected her to have anything to confess. She swallowed and took his hand.

"I set you up on some really stinky dates."

David laughed.

"It's okay. It all worked out in the end, didn't it? You more than made up for it." He squeezed her hand. He didn't get it. Emily shook her head.

"No, I mean, I set you up on those dates… on purpose," she said, looking at him apologetically. David's brows knitted together as his eyes narrowed at her.

"Okay…."

"The investors… oh gosh, this is hard to explain without sounding like a jerk." She took a breath. "Right. Okay, I'm just going to say it." She raised her right hand and pulled out the metal clasp that was digging into her scalp. Her hair fell past her shoulders and she shook her head in relief.

"Just before you came into my office, I had a call with the investors. They told me that they wouldn't invest in the expansion of my business because I wasn't married—as though I didn't truly understand being a matchmaker without being married. So, I needed a husband," she said in one breath. David moved his hand away from hers and studied her for a moment. She nervously ran her tongue across the back of her teeth and watched him carefully. Was he mad? Did he understand? She couldn't tell.

"And, I came in saying I needed a wife in thirty days and that seemed to be the perfect opportunity for you," he looked up at the car ceiling with his jaw clenched. He was mad.

"I'm so sorry, David." Tears were filling Emily's eyes as she looked at him imploringly. David turned to her and shook his head.

"You have nothing to be sorry about," he said quickly. Emily raised her brows. The anger on his face was gone and he was holding her hand again.

"Really? Did you even hear what I said?" She couldn't read him. Was he hiding something from her?

"It seems like a pretty big coincidence, don't you think?" he said in a low voice.

"Maybe it was supposed to be that way," Emily mused. David raised a hand to her face and caressed her cheek with his thumb.

"You're really not mad at me?" she asked softly, hardly able to believe that the truth was finally out and David wasn't acting like she was the biggest traitor on the planet.

He looked at her with the purest eyes; his lips were apart slightly, then he licked the bottom one and glanced down at hers.

"If we're doing confessions, then I should tell you that from the day we first met, I fantasied about being with you."

Emily gulped. An explosion of excitement was going on inside her body. She leaned in and kissed him gently. The rising passion within drove her to keep going. She wrapped her arms around his shoulders and he clutched her back.

Everything was going to be okay. David knew the truth and set her free. Not only that, but now he was kissing her back. This would just be a funny story to tell the grandkids, she thought.

As their hands roamed, the flush of heat rose to

Emily's cheeks, and it was only when the car came to an abrupt stop that the two of them broke apart, panting. They stared at each other, shoulders heaving up and down, needing a few moments to catch their breaths. Then they burst into laughter.

"We just got married," Emily said, grinning this time. The realization sent pulses of electricity through her. David grinned back.

"Yes, we did."

CHAPTER EIGHTEEN

MEET THE FAMILY

D avid nestled back into the soft leather armchair as the jet engines rumbled into life. He glanced over in amusement at Emily as she was looking around the flight cabin, taking it all in.

"You know, technically this is half yours now," he said with a grin. Emily's mouth fell open and she raised her eyebrows.

"You have your own private jet? Most people hire one out."

David rubbed his chin and scratched the hairs of his five o' clock shadow. He watched her fasten her seatbelt and clutch the arms of her chair. The skin over her knuckles turned white.

"How long is this flight?" she asked, in a fake nonchalant way. David noticed her biting her lip and the fixed smile on her face wasn't fooling him at all.

"Are you a nervous flyer?" He reached out a hand and placed it on top of hers.

"No," Emily replied a little too quickly.

David cocked a brow and looked at her frankly.

"Oh? Then why are your hands clammy? Is there something else making you nervous? You seemed okay in the helicopter." He traced the line of her knuckles with his index finger and touched the huge diamond ring on her wedding finger.

"I just hate the take-off and landing."

The plane sped along the runway and the engines' roar flooded the cabin. David watched the color fade from Emily's cheeks as she shut her eyes. He patted his legs wondering what he could do to distract her as the plane set off into the sky. Then an idea came to mind and he grinned.

"Hey, I want to give you something," he said as he tugged on Emily's hand. She opened her eyes and stared at him, a pool of sweat glistened on her upper lip. David reached into his pocket and retrieved a small rectangular box.

"This is yours." He handed the box to Emily, who took it into her shaking hands.

"What is it?" She flipped open the box and gasped. The plane leveled off and the push of the engines normalized as Emily stared at the contents inside the box.

"I can't believe it," she said barely above a whisper.

David cracked his knuckles and watched her eyes tearing up.

"Do you like it?" he asked with anticipation. Emily threw her head back and laughed.

"Is that a serious question?" she pulled out a piece of jewelry. It was the sunflower necklace he had seen her wearing in Oliver's store.

"You really shouldn't have." Emily shot him a look. "It's too much."

"Call it a wedding gift."

Emily held it out to him, the line of sunflower jewels sparkled in the rays of sunshine coming in through the round window, dazzling David.

"Will you help me put it on?" She turned her back to him and swept her hair to the side. David fumbled with the necklace, attempting to fasten the delicate clasp. Once he was done, Emily turned back and beamed at him, her hand touched the necklace as if it were made of glass.

"I love it" was all she said.

I love you David thought, staring into Emily's sparkling eyes. He moved forward to brush her hair away from her face and caress her cheek, but the plane shook and Emily's happy resolve turned back into blind panic.

"What was that?" she said, holding onto the arm rests for dear life.

"It's all right, it's just a bit of a turbulence," David reassured her. He unfastened his belt and knelt down at Emily's feet, placing his hands on hers.

"Emily, you didn't tell me you were afraid of flying. I'm sorry."

"I'm not usually. I'm… Is it me, or is it really hot in here? I'm fine, really." Emily pulled on the neckline of her dress. David resisted the urge to roll his eyes. Instead, he took her hands and held them tightly.

"You're adorable. You know that, right?"

A tiny smile crept across her face in response.

"There we go, touch down," David said in a soothing tone. The plane came to a stop and David took his eyes away from the window and looked at Emily who was visibly shaken in her seat. Thankfully, it was a short flight to Martha's Vineyard.

Emily sat bolt upright and smoothed out her dress. "Thank goodness," she said with a sigh of relief.

David stood and held out his hand for her.

"We need to get you a drink."

Emily took his hand and the two of them made their way to the hatch. David glanced back at her periodically as they descended the metal steps to the ground. He wondered how she walked in those high heels. Despite her panic on the flight, she was putting on her confident act. She smiled breezily and flicked her hair back over her shoulder once they reached the ground.

A tall man, who some could mistake as himself, stood afar off. He raised a cut crystal highball to them as they approached.

"Nice to see you, baby brother," he said, then broke into a smile and his nostrils flared as they locked eyes.

"Edward," David replied curtly. They shook hands briefly before his brother turned to Emily.

"And this must be your mysterious wife?" He held out his hand for Emily. She squared her shoulders and shook his hand firmly. David smiled. She was used to dealing with rich, entitled men. His older brother was no exception.

"I'm Emily, nice to finally meet David's mysterious brother." Her response almost had David snort.

171

Good comeback.

They were standing on a small runway, and in the distance, David could see a glimpse of the summer house.

"Well, I'd love to stay here and continue this pleasant conversation, but I'm sorry to say, we do not have the luxury of time." Edward turned and opened the car door to the Rolls Royce beside them.

"Time to see our dying grandmother."

David clenched his jaw so hard he thought his teeth might crumble. He took Emily's hand; this time it was his palms that were sweaty. Emily was completely composed. *How does she do that?*

Freak out one minute, then act cool and collected the next. He noted that Emily was holding his hand protectively. He appreciated the squeeze and her meaningful glance as they got into the car. She didn't need to verbalize the words: *I'm here for you.*

Edward gestured to the small woman sitting in the back with them. "Catherine, you remember my brother? This is his lovely wife, Emma—"

"Emily." David cut in. He glared at his brother, who sneered back at him. Edward's eyes glinted, as his face twisted into a devilish grin.

Emily shook hands with Edward's wife, then the women struck up a polite conversation, but David could not hear it; his ears were ringing and he ground his teeth.

Despite being close in age, their personalities could not be further apart. David was artistic and introverted. Edward was outspoken and analytical. David always wanted to do what was right for the family. Edward only cared about himself. Edward was not always selfish. The two of them used to be close, but his character changed when it was announced that he would inherit the entire family fortune.

They had not been in such close vicinity since the night Edward revealed his master plan.

"Father, David… I am glad you are both here, so that I can announce this to you simultaneously." He spread his arms out wide and puffed out his chest proudly. *They were standing in the private balcony of a theatre. His wife Catherine was the lead singer in the opera and it was opening night. The show had ended and people were starting to leave. It was now Edward's turn to take center stage and make a disturbing announcement.*

"As you know, I am to receive the remainder of Grandmother's shares of the company," he began matter-of-factly, as if it was not unreasonable or surprising. David and his father stared at him blankly.

"I wanted to make it clear that I have come to a decision regarding the direction I want to take the family name." He lowered his arms and took a formal stance clasping his hands

together in front of him. "I am going to sell the Marks hotel chain. I already have a potential buyer."

David glanced over at his father, who remained quiet but the color drained from his face. He just stared at Edward, perhaps waiting for him to shout, "Got you! Just kidding. I'd never do that to the family name!" But that didn't happen.

David got to his feet. "You want to sell us out? Does Grandmother know?"

Edward looked back at him frankly. "One word: Vegas."

David and his father glanced at each other. "What?" they said in unison.

"I want a casino."

"Then buy a casino, you don't need to sell the entire Marks hotel chain to do that." His father got to his feet and sighed.

"No, I want to build a new Vegas. An entire city built around one giant casino." Edward spoke dramatically while moving his hands to emphasize his points. "Our name will go down in history, and not as measly hotel owners, but innovative, forward-thinkers. I'll build a whole city where only the very elite will be allowed entrance."

David had been furious—still was. The reason their grandmother was bequeathing all the company's shares to Edward was because he'd married a "respectable" woman, one who could look the part to represent the future of the Marks dynasty. Catherine was not only respectable, but sweet and seemingly level-headed.

David could not understand why she would stand by Edward's crazy plan to destroy the legacy.

He also could not understand his grandmother's wishes. Cutting his father out of the will was almost understandable... considering their history. But why would Grandmother trust Edward with everything? Did she know of his plan? If she didn't, it was too late to tell her. *Who shares such news to someone when they are dying?* Edward knew that, and he was taking advantage of the situation, which was an unfathomable change to the brother he'd always known.

With his jaw clamped together, David held the small of Emily's back as they walked into the home.

CHAPTER NINETEEN

GRANDMOTHER MARKS

Emily tried to remain composed. She allowed herself to steal a few glances around as they entered. They came into a hall, lined with work staff ready to meet them. A woman offered Emily a tray with a small facecloth that she held it with a pair of tongs. Emily shot a look at David to see him washing his hands and the back of his neck with a towel.

"Thank you," Emily said in a quiet voice to the woman, then copied David. The towel was steaming and the warmth flooded her senses as she washed her hands. *This is amazing,* she thought and resolved to microwave a wet towel each night to use before bed.

"You're here, grand. We must go in right away," Charles entered the hall and shook hands with his sons, before he kissed Catherine on her cheek.

He turned to Emily. "Lovely to see you again, my newest daughter-in-law." He pressed his lips to her cheek, Emily smiled warmly at him. He addressed her as his daughter-in-law at David's penthouse suite—back when she was merely pretending to be David's wife. This time, it was true. She was his newest daughter-in-law.

"Thank you. Do I call you Dad now?" Warmth rose to her cheeks as she said the word.

He clapped his hand on her back, just like David would do. "Charles will do just fine."

"How is she," David asked his father. Charles turned to look at him gravely.

"Not well. The nurses are saying her kidneys are failing. It could be any day now."

The group followed Charles out of the hall. Emily glanced one more time at the grand staircase, the central point of the entryway and home. She wondered how many rooms were upstairs.

They walked through to a garden room, and a realization dawned on her: she was about to meet Grandmother Marks. Not just that, but dying Grandmother Marks. She gulped. Their make-believe suddenly became very real. Could she pull this off? Would Grandmother Marks like her? Could Emily lie to a dying woman? Well, technically it was no longer a lie. Emily wriggled her fingers against the gold band on her left hand. Stirring emotions inside sent a bubble up to her chest. She glanced up at David, his jaw was clenched. He was tense. She wanted to plant tender kisses all over his face and hold him close. As if kisses could make everything better.

They walked out into a garden. It took all of Emily's self-control not to gasp. A myriad of flowers bloomed in splashes of colors. The lilies were nearly her height and the sunflowers towered above her. It was like an explosion of confetti, and one bloom had large pointy petals the size of a dinner plate. As they walked along the gravel path crunching beneath their feet, the constant musical chirping of the bird from the aviary was relaxing. Emily looked around in the blazing sunshine and thought, *If I were dying, this is where I would want to be.* They turned a corner and a summer house stood before them. It was smaller than the main building, the sides covered with climbing ivy. With the tall men in front of her, she leaned to the side to get a better look at.

The front of the house was made entirely of glass

—not a speck of dirt in sight. She wondered how many times the staff cleaned the windows to keep the glass looking like that.

The group stopped walking and Emily almost bumped into David. She clutched his arm and peered around him to see what was happening. Charles was speaking to a woman who looked like a nurse. She was dressed in blue scrubs and had an upside-down pocket watch clipped to her shirt. Emily used to have a pretend one as a kid; she loved that watch. David wrapped his arm around her shoulders. His face was somber, and his eyes glistened. A lump formed in her throat and she swallowed uncomfortably against it. This was not going to be easy.

"Come in, quietly." Charles motioned for them to follow. The collective energy changed, as though carrying an invisible weight.

"Mother, the boys are here."

"Edward? David?"

"Yes."

Emily squeezed David's arm as he let her go and followed Edward to the bed positioned in front of the bay window. Emily stood beside Catherine, who was almost a foot taller than her. The two of them looked on in absolute silence as Edward and David stooped down to offer their grandmother a kiss.

A white cat lay curled up on the edge of the bed,

sitting nose to tail. Emily looked at its dark, sorrowful eyes and wondered if the cat smelled death approaching.

"I've had a good life. Don't feel bad for me," she said to her grandsons. "Come now, none of these tears. Let me see your wives."

Emily glanced at Catherine who gave a small smile at her before marching forward. Emily followed a few steps back.

Here goes nothing. She took a breath.

"Grandmother, I'm glad I got to see you, before you go." Catherine's voice was like a songbird. She kissed the woman in the bed and smiled serenely. She appeared genuine. Emily gawped and wondered whether this was her dark sense of humor or she was just as cold-hearted as Edward. The frail woman chortled knowingly. "Yes, I'm glad to see you too, before I pop my clogs."

Emily resisted the urge to laugh at the sight of Catherine, who winked at her. Emily turned back to look at the grandmother who stretched out a hand to her.

"You are Emily. Come closer, child."

Emily stumbled forward, struggling to keep balance on her high heels now that her ankles were aching. She leaned forward and kissed the woman on her cheek.

Her waxy skin was cool and as thin as paper. Her breaths came out unevenly. Emily leaned away slightly to give her space. The elderly woman looked even smaller in person than she had on the TV.

"Lovely to meet you in person…." Emily hesitated. She wondered how to address her. Should she call her Grandmother Marks?

"Let me look at you." The woman reached out with her bony hand to grasp Emily's. Her eyes wandered up and down Emily's body, then rested on her engagement ring.

"My late husband bought me that ring shortly before he died. It's nice to see it on a much less wrinkly hand," she said. Her voice was surprisingly steady and her eyes twinkled as she grinned.

Emily gasped. David gave her the family ring? She shot a nervous look at him; he was standing near the foot of the bed and kept his gaze on his grandmother. His face was almost as pale as hers.

"Do you love him?"

Emily turned back to look at the woman, who stared imploringly into her eyes. Emily took a breath. She remembered all of the times David showed her kindness, burning his steak, coming to the dinner with the investors, taking her out on the helicopter ride. She thought about the way his cheeks dimpled as he smiled. The sheepish laugh he made when she cracked a joke, and the way he held her protectively in his arms.

She bit her lip.

"I really do." Emily's voice cracked on a flood of emotions. The last few weeks had been a whirlwind. Her job was to match the perfect couple and watch them fall in love. She had been a part of that for years, but she never expected it to happen to her, and certainly not so quickly. Could she pinpoint the moment she knew she loved David? Not really. But at this moment, at his grandmother's bedside, she knew. The knowledge burned inside of her being, so much so she wanted to scream.

I love David.

The thought came so freely. So simply. It were as if the fact had been there all along.

"And you promise not to betray him? You know what happened to his father, don't you?" Emily glanced back at David again, who shifted his weight but did not look at her.

"Married the wrong woman. Without a prenup, either. David tells me he doesn't believe in a prenup. He's a romantic, just like his father." Grandmother's words were flying out of her mouth now. The frail, barely breathing woman was gone, and one to be reckoned with was now in her place. "But I knew, you see. And every day I regret allowing him to marry that wretched woman." Emily gasped at the vehemence in the woman's words. "Oh but, my dear, not you. Don't you worry. I knew from our little chat the other day... You aren't afraid to tell the truth. David will always know where he stands with you. And I like that."

Emily squeezed her hands gently as her own eyes pooled with tears. It was lies. All lies. When they spoke on the phone, Emily was just playing a part, and she'd been playing David. Regret bubbled inside of her and rested in the base of her neck. Even though David now knew the truth, she'd still started their relationship on lies.

"Now, answer this for me," the grandmother continued, unaware of Emily's internal torment. "Can you imagine growing old with David?"

Her words had a warming effect on Emily, who closed her eyes and imagined them both sitting on a park bench. David would have deep laugh lines around his eyes and mouth as he smiled at her, his thin hair curling at the ears and grey with white streaks. She imagined him holding her hand, his skin warm, soft, and wrinkled. He would then raise his other hand and surprise her with a bouquet of sunflowers. "Happy Anniversary, darling," he'd say and kiss her gently on the cheek. Emily opened her eyes and tears rolled down her cheeks. Her mouth was glued shut as a bubble of emotion sat in her mouth, silencing her. There was no need to speak, though. Grandmother Marks studied her face and gave a nod.

"I thought so."

CHAPTER TWENTY

An Eventful Night

"Julie, open the doors. I want to feel the air on my face." The nurse bowed to Grandmother Marks and rolled back the glass doors. A gust of cool air flooded the bedroom and the group shivered against it. The day had cooled off as the sun set behind the trees. They had been with Grandmother for hours and time seemed to stand still inside the room, but the outside world kept moving.

"Your rooms are ready, and I've arranged for you all to have a party tonight, some of my friends will be joining us."

"Are you feeling well enough to entertain?" Charles asked.

"Well, like the old saying, 'it's now or never.' I choose now."

The group began to leave. But not before David heard Grandmother say, "Call my lawyer," to one of the staff. David caught sight of Charles, who give him a pointed look.

"Hey." He rubbed Emily's back to catch her attention. Edward and Catherine walked ahead talking to each other in low voices.

"Yes?"

"You go ahead. I've got to talk to my father."

Emily nodded and followed the others. He watched her go, momentarily hypnotized at the sight of her hips swaying with every step. He shook his head. *Snap out of it.*

"Come on," Charles murmured and the two of them walked down to the aviary. The high-pitched chirping of the birds was sure to drown out their quiet conversation.

"It's done. You can relax now."

David snorted. "You mean, *you* can."

Charles raised his brows at him but decided to remain quiet. "She seems to be quite taken with you. I don't know how you did it so fast. But I always believed in you."

David's heart panged, like someone just struck a chord and the sound echoed in his head. Emily had been giving off signals all day. The furtive glances, clutching his arm, rubbing his back. And then there was the way she got emotional at Grandmother Marks' questions. She changed from the ultra-confident, sassy businesswoman he met in her office two weeks ago. She was quieter, less sure of herself and clearly outside her comfort zone. Yet behind the nerves, her smile made her eyes sparkle and the warmth of her touch sent tingles through his senses.

"Do you love her? You think you're going to make it work?" Charles' words snapped David out of his thoughts.

"I do."

Just those words, coupled with thoughts of Emily, warmed his heart and gave him hope for their future.

Charles clapped his son on the back and offered a chuckle. "Looks like it's worked out for everyone, then. You won't tell her about our arrangement, will you?"

David shook his head. What use would it be now? Did it matter his father set them up? Is that really a big deal? Now that they had feelings for one another... didn't that change things? Charles smiled and gave a nod.

"Good. Well, I'll let you go back to your wife. We'll see you at the party."

The grin on David's face grew wider. *My wife. That's right, Emily is my wife now.* He hurried along the path back to the house, his mind playing out scenarios that made his mouth dry.

Davild knocked on his bedroom door. He knew which room Emily would be in. Being married, they were expected to share a room, of course. And this was his childhood bedroom. The one he would stay in during the summer holidays when he visited his grandmother.

"Yes," Emily's muffled voice carried through the door. David pushed the handle down and opened it. Emily stood across the room barefoot and her hair cascaded down to her narrow waist. David wanted to scoop her up into his arms and carry her to the four-poster bed. His face heated at the thought.

"Hi," Emily said as she tucked a piece of hair behind her ear. David closed the door and stood there, wondering what to do.

"Hi" was all he could say. For the first time since they said "I Do" they were alone in a room. But theirs was a marriage of convenience. Emily did it to help him out, how did she feel about it? He sighed. The day had been long and was far from over. Soon, the two of them would have to make their appearance at a party in the garden with all of Grandmother Marks' closest friends. All he wanted to do was take Emily to bed and have their own private party.

"So… that was intense." Emily's soft voice dragged David out of his head. She tilted her head to the side and surveyed him sympathetically. "How are you feeling?"

David swallowed. His brain was foggy and he couldn't process all of the thoughts and feelings swirling around inside. It was intense. The reality that his grandmother was dying had still not set in. Her health had been a long and arduous decline. Between his father being so pragmatic about it, and Edward already spending his inheritance, his whole family was falling apart. Was everyone just burying their heads in the sand and refusing to face up to reality of the situation? Their grandmother was going to die. The family used to be so close, and she held everyone together. She arranged all the family events. She took the most interest in how everyone was. She cared. Then she made the dramatic decision to change her will, leaving everything to Edward and it was as if an atom bomb hit the family. And everyone just seemed to be very matter-of-fact about it all.

Seeing her looking so weak, watching her talk to Emily, holding her hands, and smiling at the ring sent a flurry of emotion through his senses. It took all of David's resolve not to crash to his knees and weep. The agony of knowing his brother planned to destroy her legacy and spend the family fortune on a pipedream was becoming too much. While visiting her in her sunny cottage, he'd been unable to look at Edward; it was hard enough reining in the satisfying thoughts of punching him in the gut and telling him he was a heartless, disloyal fool, who only cared about himself. So instead, he kept his eyes fixated on Grandmother.

Emily. Just saying her name had hope blossoming within him like a sunflower. Emily spoke so softly and held his grandmother's hands tenderly. She didn't move back in repulsion. Even Catherine appeared awkward and glanced at the door, probably planning her escape. But Emily remained present and caring. His heart swelled at the thought. David jumped and blinked at the touch of her hand on his arm.

"Are you okay?" Emily was standing on tip toes and looking at him with her hands rubbing his arms. Her eyes were dark and sorrowful. Seeing her looking at him with pity broke his resolve and the dam burst.

He knelt down and his shoulders heaved up and down as he cried. Emily knelt down with him, wrapping her arms around his neck. David buried his head in her hair with his cheek pressed up against her shoulder.

David's grief eased as he felt her hair against his skin and inhaled the scent of Emily's perfume on her neck. Slowly, he raised a hand and took a handful of her hair, kissing a line up her neck to her jaw. Emily leaned back, forcing him to let go of her hair and see the bewilderment on her face.

"What are you doing?"

David wiped his eyes and shook his head with a laugh.

"I don't know," he replied honestly. What was he doing? One minute he was crying, the next he was kissing her. But all he knew, was in that moment he didn't want to think anymore. He didn't want to process what was going on. He didn't care about family politics or what happened next. He just wanted Emily. He wanted to hold her, caress her, kiss her. He just wanted to be with her. Was that wrong? Emily seemed to be following his thoughts. She sighed and pulled on his hands as she got to her feet.

"Come on," she said as he stood. "We need to get you presentable. I heard the kitchen staff saying that guests will be arriving soon." Emily ran across the room and gestured to the black suit lying on the bed.

"You'll feel better if you take a quick shower, then you can wear this," she added.

"I'd feel better if you joined me."

Emily's cheeks reddened.

CHAPTER TWENTY-ONE

Burning Desire

Emily forced a smile with her hands on her hips as she watched David walk into the bathroom. His neck was blotchy and his shoulders slumped, a start contrast to his usually casual smile and straight posture. Her heart ached to see him this way. Once the door closed she lowered herself onto the bed in a daze. Tears flooded her vision at the memory of David in her arms, trembling. He was quiet, and if it wasn't for his tears wetting the neckline of her dress, she could have guessed he was laughing. It seemed like years had passed since their conversation in the limousine. With the burden of her secret lifted, and David not being mad about it, there was a sense of relief. Yet, something jabbed at her insides, though she couldn't work out what. David was in a vulnerable place mentally. She wondered how best to deal with that. Her thoughts battled as she shimmied out of her dress. A long pastel purple gown lay on the bed next to David's tux. She ran her fingers down the organza material and carefully unzipped it. The sound of the door banging against the wall caused Emily to spin on the spot and stare, open-mouthed at a dripping wet David, in nothing but the world's tiniest towel. The two of them gawped at each other, then Emily burst out laughing. Forgetting that she was wearing nothing but a white satin slip, she dropped the dress.

"That was the world's fastest shower," she said between breaths. She had to gasp for air after laughing so hard. "Why are you wearing a face cloth?"

David's face grew crimson red as he clutched the towel protecting what was left of his modesty.

"There aren't any towels in the bathroom." He sidled toward the closet. Grinning sheepishly at her, Emily roared. In fact, she laughed so hard, she creased over clutching the splitting pain in her side as she fell onto the bed.

"You look—"

"Sexy?"

Emily eyed him. His body glistened in the golden

sunset streaming through the windows, which softened the lines of his muscles. Yes, he did look sexy. But the miniscule square of cotton had her rolling around on the bed with laughter again.

"That is the funniest thing I've seen all year!" She sat up and looked down at the dress laying discarded on the bed. David disappeared behind the door of the closet and Emily took the opportunity to pull on the dress in a swift movement. She was bending her arms back like a contortionist when David reappeared, this time with a large white towel wrapped around his waist. Suddenly, the sight of him was far less amusing and a lot more thrilling.

"Do you need help with that?" His voice was low and silky as he swaggered across the room, toward her. Emily's cheeks warmed as she eyed him, closing the space between them.

"I've managed to dress myself perfectly well for the last twenty-five years," Emily said defiantly as her fingers slipped over the zipper. David rolled his eyes and ran his hand through his wet hair.

"Turn around," he said with a sigh. Emily gulped. She lowered her hands and slowly spun to face away from him.

Two hands gently grasped her dress from the back and pulled as the zipper rose to her neck.

"There," David whispered softly. He swept her hair

away from her neck, and the touch of his lips against her skin sent shivers down her spine. Emily turned around and looked up at him. She wondered if his skin was on fire; the heat radiating off his body flooded her senses and she bit her lip against the rush of excitement growing within her.

It would have been so easy to throw her arms around his neck and give into her instinctive urges.

"We got married today," David's low voice vibrated through Emily's body. She inhaled the menthol from his body wash and held her breath.

"Sorry Mr. and Mrs. Marks, the door was ajar. I did knock."

Emily and David jumped away from each other and looked in the direction of the apologetic voice by the door. A short elderly man dressed in a black suit bowed to them both.

"Martin. It's great to see you again," David said as he strolled over to the man. Martin's face creased as he grinned back. Neither of them appeared to be abashed by David's towel sarong.

"And you, Mr. Marks. Congratulations, we were all very happy to hear about your news." He beamed at Emily, which she took as a cue to walk up to him.

"Hello," she said as she held out her hand. Martin hesitated and glanced at David for approval before he tentatively took her hand. "Please, call me

Emily. It's nice to meet you, Martin." The look of surprise on Martin's face told her that it was not common for the service staff to be spoken to so directly. He gave a furtive look at David who nodded reassuringly.

"Thank you, Mrs... Emily." He cleared his throat after they shook hands and turned back to David.

"I have come to tell you that the party is about to begin."

David and Emily exchanged looks.

"I thought it wasn't going to start for another hour, at least."

Martin shuffled his feet and looked to the floor. "Mrs. Marks... senior, is anxious to begin, now that her guests have arrived."

David nodded to him and Martin slowly vacated the room, closing the door behind him. David turned to Emily.

"I guess we need to be quick, then." He grasped her hands but she stepped away, keeping a safe distance between them.

"David," she said in a warning tone. Despite her attempt at giving him a hard look, a bubble of laughter escaped her lips. David rubbed the back of his neck and grinned, his face flushed with color.

"Right. I'm going to touch up my hair and make-up in the bathroom while you get dressed." She wagged a finger at him as she spoke and pointed at the clothes lying on the bed.

"You sure I shouldn't go down like this?" David asked, sashaying his hips side to side with a grin. The towel loosened and he grabbed it just before it fell. Emily threw her head back and laughed as she marched to the bathroom. She turned and just before she closed the door, caught David's eye, still grinning at her with his head tilted to the side. Her heart swelled.

A s Emily did the finishing touches to her make-up, there was a knock on the door. A young woman dressed in uniform politely offered to take her to David, who had gone down to meet the guests. Emily slipped on her favorite pair of Jimmy Choo shoes, secured the sunflower necklace around her neck, and followed the woman out of the room.

The sky was dark, but the blanket of darkness gave way to a huge mass of twinkling stars. Emily was over-whelmed the moment she stepped out into the veranda. There was a large crowd of well-dressed men and women talking together in quiet tones. A string quartet played in front of a large fountain, and servers walked around the guests with silver platters, handing out drinks and appetizers. Emily craned her neck to catch a sight of David, but could not see him anywhere. None of the guests appeared to be aware of her arrival; she was able to turn and follow the small path toward the summer house unnoticed. Perhaps David was speaking to his grandmother. As she rounded the corner to the home, the screeching birds alerted her arrival.

"Is that you, Emily?"

Emily peered through the dim lighting to see a tall figure walking toward her. The person stooped down and kissed her on the cheek. Emily thought for a moment it was David, but the bristles of his beard gave him away.

"Edward, where is Catherine?"

"She's off talking to the Sultan of wherever. He's a fan of the opera, you see." He offered his arm. "Walk with me?" Even though he said it like a question, he did not wait, but began to walk them down toward the aviary. Emily slid her hand into the crook of his arm and took care not to land on any cracks in the path.

"My brother has good taste," Edward said silkily. His teeth glowed white as he grinned at her. Emily wondered if he was trying to pay her a compliment. "I hope you understand, when I first heard about your marriage, I was concerned."

"Oh?" Emily tried to sound innocent, but part of

her was beginning to panic. *Here we go.* She had a feeling someone in the family wouldn't buy their situation.

"I know my baby brother, and he doesn't make a decision… quickly." Edward appeared to be choosing his words carefully. Emily remained quiet, sensing he had more to say. "When we were kids, and we'd go to the zoo, David would agonize for *ages* over what toy to get in the gift shop. I remember he spent forty minutes unable to choose between a giraffe plushie and a tiger yo-yo." He chuckled. "Father told him he could get both, of course, but David follows rules. He was supposed to choose."

Emily chewed her lip with a nervous smile. Getting married in secret, out of the blue, would be weird behavior from most people. But for David, clearly, this was totally out of character. Add to that, the fact it would scupper his brother's inheritance, it was a sticky situation. Emily surreptitiously looked around the garden for David's familiar form. Or anyone, for that matter.

"Yes, David used to be indecisive, but now not so much," she said thoughtfully as walked further into the garden. Edward gave an awkward laugh.

"Touché," he said. "I can see why he's so fond of you."

He stopped walking and Emily dropped her hand

and stood away from him a little. The evening chill had her holding her arms.

"I'm just curious," Edward said. His voice had a dangerous tone to it. She knew those three simple words were going to lead to difficult questions. She stiffened and held her breath. The party of guests were well outside of earshot now, and David was nowhere to be seen. Emily wondered whether to feign illness or run away screaming. Instead, she stood rooted on the spot.

"Why would David lie to his dying grandmother, telling her that he just got married?"

There it was. The words smacked her in the face as if he physically hit her. Emily's brain went into overdrive. She set her jaw and reverted back to her training. Difficult conversations happened all the time at work. Heartbroken women weeping in her office, over the callous men who had convinced them of their love, only to find they were dating several women at the same time. Furious men who were stood up. The complaints were endless. She imagined that Edward was just another dissatisfied client who needed to be dealt with professionally. The first step; validation.

"You're right," she said firmly. Edward stood immobile, but the twitch of his head told her he was listening. She took a breath and resolved to tell the truth—sort of. "David and I were not married when he told the family. I think it's like you say, he doesn't usually jump into anything too quickly. He didn't want the family to change his mind."

"Why would we—"

"Let me finish," Emily said curtly. Edward closed his mouth and folded his arms. This gave her more confidence. "It was a whirlwind, I'll grant you that." That was the truth. "But when you know, you know."

"So, I'm supposed to believe that this is all about love at first sight, and nothing to do with my grand-mother's inheritance? You are aware, I presume, that now David is married, he will receive a portion of her estate?"

"Careful, it sounds like you're accusing your brother—"

"Maybe I'm more suspicious of you and your intentions," Edward cut in.

"Are you calling me a—"

"Desperate gold-digging woman who saw an opportunity and—"

Whack. Edward stopped talking and moaned, as something—or someone, had punched him on the cheekbone.

"Stay away from my wife. You don't have any right." David's words set a fire alight within Emily and she couldn't stop her face from breaking into a smile. David and Edward had a silent standoff, their shoulders squared and fists clenched. Their eyes glinted dangerously in the lighting. Emily wasn't sure if they were going to fight or walk away.

"I was only congratulating Emily on joining the family. She seems very happy—considering the circumstances."

David raised his fist, but Edward lifted his palms up in defeat.

"All right, I'm going. But this isn't over."

"Oh, yes it is," Emily said with her hands on her hips. She gave him a steely stare. A triumphant smile flashed across Edward's face and his eyes flitted between David and Emily. It was as if this moment was part of his plan. Why would he be pleased? Emily wondered as she watched him wave a hand and walk away without another word. David turned and pulled Emily in for a tight hug.

"I'm sorry you had to go through that." His voice was smooth and gentle again. Emily broke away and looked at him.

"I was okay, you know. I can stand up for myself."

David laughed. "I know," he said as he took her hand, and they walked farther down the path away from the house. "But what he said was—"

"Absolutely true," Emily said simply. David stopped walking, Emily followed and turned to him. "When you came in and told me you needed a wife, it couldn't have been at a more convenient time. If I believed in that sort of thing, I would have called it Fate."

"But you weren't looking for my money...."

"Maybe not, but you were the key to getting those investors onboard. And I put my ambition ahead of your feelings. I owe you an apology for that. I'm sorry."

David clutched her hands and pressed them to his lips. The heat of his breath against her skin took out the chill in the air and Emily was basking in his warmth.

"You never need to apologize for anything," he said in a low voice. His eyes darted left and right, and Emily wondered if he wanted to say something; if he had, then he appeared to decide against it.

"I want to show you something," he mumbled and they started walking again.

CHAPTER TWENTY-TWO

Sweet, tender mercies

"Shouldn't we be getting back to the party?" Emily asked, as they hurried farther down the winding path. David's heart was pounding so fast he could hear it in his ears.

"I'm not going to subject you to anymore interrogations," he replied. The path ended and they were walking on sand now. Emily stopped for a moment to take off her shoes.

"But your grandmother—"

"She'll be fine. She's enjoying the music and the sound of everyone having fun." David looked over at

Emily, her dress flowed out at the waist and the tight bodice accentuated her curves. The sunflower necklace stood out in the dark of the night, a flash of yellow, like a line of stars on her neckline.

"My brother and I would make a den down here. There's a cave farther along the shore."

He watched Emily take in the scene before them. The moonlight flooded the still water to make it look glassy and palm trees stood like shadows in the sky. David swayed as the air moved with the tide. The water eased in and out as if the ocean were breathing. He watched Emily close her eyes and inhale deeply, taking in the salty, sea-air.

"Well, this is magical," Emily mused, opening her eyes. They glowed like two moons. David had the urge to cradle her face with his hands and kiss her. He let go of her hand and took his shoes and socks off. Emily dropped her shoes on the sand and pulled something out of her hair. The bun unraveled and her wavy hair fell in a swift motion to her waist.

"Come on." Emily picked up the ends of her dress and ran toward the water. David raised his brows as he watched her dipping her toes in and spinning around in circles. She was a beautiful silhouette, dancing in the water. He removed his jacket and tie and followed her.

"Here, you need to cool down," Emily said as she

splashed him, dropping the skirt of her dress. The water was like tiny daggers against his body; he shuddered. David thrust his hand in the water and showered Emily from head to toe.

The two of them playfully splashed one another and ran around in the shallow water for some time. David's cheeks hurt from laughing and smiling so much, but he didn't care. Within minutes, the two of them were soaked from head to toe and the cold air had them both shivering.

"You see, this is why I love you."

The words escaped David's lips before he could register them. Emily stopped splashing and stood still, staring at him.

"You love me?" she asked.

David's defences fell away. He had never been sure of anything in his life, always second-guessing everything, always wondering if he was doing what was "right." But being with Emily felt natural—who he'd been missing all along. Even in all the chaos, the lies, the politics… Emily made him feel grounded, safe, and sure.

"I want to make this work," he said as he took her hand. He held it to his chest and stared at her imploringly. There was no time to wonder if she would freak out and reject him. Or if he was being too forward.

They got married, didn't they? She agreed to that. They'd spent more time together in the last few weeks than he ever had with his family. Yet, it wasn't enough. He wanted more time with her. He never wanted to be away from Emily again.

"Do you think we can?"

David crouched and lifted her up in his arms. She cried out in shock from the cold, and laughed as she wrapped her arms around his neck. "What are you doing?" she asked through giggles. David carried her easily, walking back toward the house.

"Isn't it tradition for a man to carry his bride over the threshold?"

"Wait—wait. Put me down," Emily ordered. David lowered her and she stood eyeing him carefully. "You mean it? You want to be married to me, for real?"

She sounded hopeful. David thought his thumping heart might burst out of his chest.

Yes, for real. I'm never letting you go.

"If you will have me."

Emily grabbed David's neck and pulled him down. He happily allowed it, and Emily captured his lips with a kiss. All the barriers that had kept them apart, came crashing down as the two of them explored each other. They broke away gasping and Emily grinned at him.

"You were saying something about a threshold?"

David picked her up again, the two of them laughing and he practically ran back up to the house.

David woke up in a state of confusion. What day was it? Why was he aching in places he didn't know could ache? Why was he ravenously hungry? Where was his shirt? He rubbed his eyes and sat up in the four-poster bed and looked around the room. Had he been dreaming? Was last night an extension of his previous fantasies?

Weak sunlight poured in through the white curtains and he stared at the black gown, water-stained and creased, laying on a chair by the window. He blinked away the sleep in his eyes and looked at the bathroom door as it opened. Emily walked in, her cheeks were rosy and her hair was completely wild. Curly, wavy, and frizzing at the hairline. She paraded around barefoot in a blue shirt that came to her knees.

"Hey, that's my favorite shirt," David said with feigned indignance.

"Oh I'm sorry, I had no idea." She sauntered over to the bed. "Do you want it back?"

"Yes, I do," David said, he no longer cared about his aches and pains. Emily placed her hands on her hips and gave him a mischievous smile.

"Well, you'll have to come and get it."

David threw the sheets off and crawled across the bed like a lion.

"Challenge accepted."

Emily squealed as he wrestled her back onto the bed.

CHAPTER TWENTY-THREE

THE TRUTH COMES OUT

Emily walked her fingers up David's chest as she lay propped up on an elbow.

"What did you think of me when we first met?"

She watched David heave a big sigh and wipe the sweat from his brow.

"I thought"—he sat up and Emily cozied up to his chest with his arm wrapped around her—"that you were the most beautiful woman I had ever seen."

Emily snuggled closer into David. They basked in the glow of their love, finally the world was right. They were together, nothing could tear them apart. She planted kisses in a line up his chest. She wanted to kiss him, every part, for all her days. Falling in love had never been so sweet. So tender. She thought she might smile until her dying day.

"I thought you were the tallest man I'd ever seen," she quipped back.

David hummed. "We should go downstairs and get some breakfast."

"Oh, someone has been working up an appetite," Emily said coyly. David nodded, his face was still red.

"I'm starving."

Emily rolled over and huffed as she looked up at the impossibly high ceiling. "I wish we could stay in here forever."

"It would get pretty boring," David said.

Emily rolled onto her side and looked him, offended. "Oh really?"

David's face turned a deeper shade of red. "Erm, I'd die of starvation?"

Emily rolled her eyes at her new husband. "Let's get food sent up to the room." She didn't want to see anyone else, especially not Edward. Was his face bruised and what story did he tell the rest of the family?

"This isn't a hotel, you know," David said with a laugh. She tilted her head at him.

"Yeah, but I'm sure your staff wouldn't mind bringing food to the room."

David sighed and got up out of bed. "We should go. We missed the whole party," he said as he got dressed.

"You didn't seem to care last night." Emily fluttered her lashes at him as she flashed her pearly whites. David bent over and rested his palms on the bed. Emily crawled up to him and planted a soft kiss on his lips.

"Hmmm," he murmured as he kissed her back. "As much as I would love to spend the day in bed with you, darling, we need to make an appearance. I want to check in on my grandmother." David's words dulled Emily's excitement; she had forgotten why they were there. His grandmother was dying. She nodded and dragged herself out of bed.

"Okay, I'll take a quick shower."

Emily held David's hand as she followed him down the grand staircase to the side door that opened out to the dining room.

"Good morning, everyone," David said brightly. Emily smiled sheepishly, clutching David's hand as she looked around the room, which had become eerily quiet. Charles sat at the head of the mahogany table, Edward and Catherine were on either side of him, and several couples joined them, all no longer enjoying their cooked breakfast. The air was surprisingly frosty, and Emily noted that all scowling faces were directed at her.

"What's wrong?" David asked, apparently sensing the odd vibes in the room. Charles sighed heavily and lifted a remote control. A large screen TV came to life on the wall across from them and Emily's mouth fell open as she stared at a picture of herself on the screen.

"Emily Stewart's fake marriage to billionaire heir David Marks is now claimed to be the biggest scandal of 2019."

The news reporters were discussing the headline. "Why do you think Emily Stewart was so happy to participate in a fake marriage?"

"Well, Linda, our source tells us that she was looking to expand her business to Los Angeles."

"Did your source have any information on how the fake marriage came about?"

"Yes, Jon. It's reported that David Marks, the younger son, would not inherit part of the family fortune unless he found a wife."

A chair scraped across the floor and Emily looked to see Edward at his feet, a dark green bruise covered his right cheek.

"I knew it," he growled. Catherine covered her mouth with her hands and stared at them both with wide eyes.

Charles switched the TV off. Emily wanted the ground to open and swallow her whole. The truth was out.

"You believe everything you hear on the news?" David began with a shrug in an attempt to sound nonchalant. "Come on, it's just sensationalist gossip."

"So, you're not opening up a matchmaking business in LA?" Edward asked Emily, his eyes burned through her soul and she swallowed nervously. Judgment day had arrived.

"Yes," she said in a quiet voice. Edward raised a hand and scoffed with exasperation.

"And how exactly did you meet David?"

Emily clung to David's hand as if her life depended on it. She glanced at him anxiously.

"He came into my office." She shifted her weight and avoided eye contact with everyone in the room. David squeezed her hand.

"None of it matters. We love each other, and we've made a commitment."

"Love." Edward snorted and paced the room. Several of the guests made their excuses and took the opportunity to escape the awkward conversation.

"We'll leave you to it. I want to see how Iris is

doing." An elderly woman patted David's arm as she followed her husband out of the room. After a few tense minutes, only Charles and Edward remained at the table. Catherine made excuses about needing to warm up for an upcoming recital for Grandmother Marks.

"I thought I could smell a rat," Edward sneered. David lunged forward but Emily pulled on his hand to stop him from strangling his brother. Charles got to his feet and the brothers looked at him.

"Enough. You two need to keep a low profile while we clear up this mess." Charles rubbed his jawline and appeared to be deep in thought. His reaction confused Emily. Was he not furious like Edward? Based on what they'd seen on TV, he should be angry.

"Oh right, I get it." Edward slammed a fist on the table. "This is perfect for you." He pointed an accusing finger at his father. "I should have known you would have had something to do with this."

"He had nothing to do with it, actually." Emily squared up to Edward and set her jaw, staring him down. Edward turned to her and laughed, shaking his head.

"You might believe that," he began, wagging a finger now at Emily, then at David. "But you're wrong. There are too many coincidences."

Emily looked at Charles who was staring at David

intently. Then she looked back at David who was chewing his lip. It was as if they were having a silent conversation.

"What are you talking about?"

"None of it matters," David began. Emily put her hands on her hips.

"What are you talking about?" she repeated firmly. She knew they shouldn't have left their bedroom, something was about to happen that would ruin everything, she could feel it.

Charles sighed and motioned for them to take a seat. "Edward, calm down. There's nothing anyone can do about it now."

Edward pressed the palms of his hands against the brick fireplace and bowed his head low for a moment.

"I'll tell Grandmother. This is wrong. *She's* a fraud." He turned and gave Emily a steely glare. Emily frowned back. She was not a fraud. Had she not told David the truth?

"It doesn't matter, Edward. They're married...." Charles glanced at David for a moment. "You did make it official, I gather? I didn't tell you to pretend to marry her."

Emily's ears began to ring.

"I'm sorry," she blurted out and took her hand away from David's grasp. He looked down at her, biting his lip so hard she was sure it would draw blood.

"What does that mean... You didn't tell David to pretend to marry me?"

Edward turned around to face them and broke into a fit of dark laughter. "Oh perfect. Just perfect." He slammed his fist on the table. "This is complete fraud. I'll get my lawyers on this. You won't see a penny of the inheritance."

"You think I'm going to stand by and let you sell the family business, and use our good name to fund your childish ambitions?" David puffed out his chest, looking at Edward furiously.

"I am the only person in this family who can make hard business decisions." Edward's voice rose a pitch and his cheeks flushed. The bruise turned a shade of purple. "You lost half of everything in your name," he accused Charles, then turned to David. "And you're an architect. What do you know about running a business?"

The men broke into a heated debate, yet Emily's brain was spinning with a debate of her own. Just what did Charles mean when he said that he didn't tell David to pretend? Was there something more David had been hiding? He'd confessed from the beginning that he needed a wife to earn his inheritance. Was the "I need to find a wife in thirty days" just a ruse?

"Charles, did you target me to be David's wife?" Emily asked. Charles shot a look at Edward. If looks could kill, Edward would have been on the floor. He forced a smile at Emily.

David turned to her and grabbed her hand.

"I never lied to you. I meant everything I said last night," he said fervently. Emily turned back to look at Charles.

"One day, you'll be a parent," Charles began calmly. Edward shrugged and covered his face with his hands; a vein bulged out of his neck. "Only then, will you understand."

Emily placed her hands on her hips again and backed away from David. "What did you do?" she asked Charles in a deathly whisper.

"What I had to… just like you," Charles shot back. Emily shook her head and stared wide-eyed at David. The color had drained from his face, and while he glanced back in her direction, he was unable to look her in the eye.

"You knew I was looking for investors didn't you? It was the perfect opportunity."

David shook his head. "It's not like that, Emily. What does it matter how we met? I love you."

Charles clapped his hand on David's shoulder. "You make each other happy, everyone can see that. Besides, you are not entirely innocent in this, are you, Emily? Did you not pursue David for your own financial agenda? Let's put the past behind us, shall we?"

Emily opened her mouth, but no sound came out. So, David and his father specifically chose her to be his wife. He'd never come in to find a "real" wife; it had been set up all along. *I guess we're both as bad as each other,* she thought.

Was David right? Did it matter? She loved him now—didn't she?

A knock on the door interrupted her thoughts and Emily gawped to see two men walk into the room—the investors from dinner.

"What are—"

Charles looked sheepish for the first time.

"Ah, yes. You have met before. Emily, this is Adam and Tyler."

"I thought—" Emily couldn't finish her sentence. What did she think? To see the two men in such an unexpected setting had her taken aback. Nothing was making any sense. The mysterious investors were friends with Charles? Is that how he knew about Emily?

"Adam and Tyler are my personal security."

The words shot through Emily's chest like a bullet. "I'm sorry, I'm confused. Then who is investing in my business? Matthew said—"

"Matthew is an old friend," Charles said calmly. A snort at the table alerted Emily that Edward was still there. He lowered his hands and shook his head. A crazed smile on his face.

"Oh it's all coming out now, the tangled web of lies you've woven." He got to his feet, looking pleased with himself. Like the detective at the end of a murder mystery novel, ready to deliver his theory with absolute accuracy.

"Haven't you worked it out yet?" he said to Emily. Grinning ear to ear, but the smile didn't reach his eyes. He pointed at his father.

"My meddling father and brother hatched a plan to steal *my* inheritance. Heaven forbid Father has to lose even more control. So, he found you. A high-profile business woman... who just so happens to be from England as well. And is on the lookout for an investment."

Edward squared his shoulders and stood by the fireplace, his hands clasped together and confident. "Father sends David in to see you. Fancy that, Emily? You need money to build your business, and in walks a billionaire who is on the lookout for a wife."

Emily frowned.

"Rich bachelors walk into my office every day," she said. "I didn't target David."

"You didn't?" Charles asked, Emily looked at him wildly. "You mean to tell me that Matthew didn't conveniently tell you to find a husband?"

Emily gawped at him and looked at David who was staring at his father and the bodyguards. He was a deer in the headlights again. She looked around at all of the men in the room and suddenly felt very small. Realization dawned on her and sank to the pit of her stomach.

"There's no deal, is there? The investors... Matthew. It was all a ploy to get me to end up with David?" She looked at David who still couldn't look at her.

"Were you ever going to tell me?" she asked. David lowered his eyes to the floor, his eyes glistening with tears. *Look at me. Why won't you look at me?* Emily paced the room now.

"I feel sick." She stopped walking. "And I want to leave." Her words brought David back to life. He nodded and turned on the spot to open the door.

"Right, let's go."

"But we're not finished, this isn't over," Edward called out. David ignored him as he held Emily's arm and they both walked out of the room.

Emily and David quietly packed their things and left the house without speaking to anyone—other than a quick goodbye to Grandmother Marks, who was sleeping. The plane ride was uneventful, and Emily sat, reeling from the conversation. There was no deal. The investors were fake. What's more, David was in on it the whole time. That's what hurt the most. How could he keep such a big secret from her? What else might he be hiding? How could she know how he felt about her?

"Take me to my apartment," she demanded of David as they exited the plane and got into the back of the limousine.

"Emily, please talk to me."

David took her hand, but she pulled away. "I can't," she said in a broken voice.

"You need to know, I had no idea about the investors."

"You've never seen your dad's bodyguards before then? Shouldn't you have recognized them?"

"No, I've never seen them. I mean, I didn't like them and I did think it was weird my father was outside the restaurant when we were there. But I didn't—"

"What?" Emily cut in. "He was there… when we were having our meeting?" Emily laughed derisively. "Perfect. So he sat outside laughing his head off, while I was making a fool of myself in front of his puppets."

"It's not like that, Emily. Really. I love you."

"You keep saying that. And every time you say it, it sounds less convincing." Emily folded her arms as her cheeks burned with rage and humiliation. All the time she had been wracked with guilt over what she did, when in truth, she played perfectly into the hand of David's father.

They pulled up outside Emily's apartment, and she didn't even wait for Henry open the door. She pushed it open and grabbed her bag from the trunk.

"Emily, wait. Please. We need to talk about this." David followed her to the door.

"Stay away from me."

"But please, Emily. We can work this out."

"I can't even look at you." Tears were flooding her vision now as she fumbled with her keys. David tried to hold her, but she shrugged him off.

"Don't touch me," she snapped. David stood back.

"Emily, please don't shut me out."

The door to the apartment building swung open and Emily threw her bag inside. She turned and just before she closed the door she paused, staring at David's crestfallen face. She pulled the platinum ring off her finger and thrust it into David's hand.

"You were never going to tell me the truth, were you?" The question was more like a statement, but she searched his face. David pressed his lips together keeping silent; she could see the internal conflict in his eyes.

No. He wasn't.

A sob escaped Emily's mouth as she closed the door, and she resolved to never look at that handsome face again.

CHAPTER TWENTY-FOUR

HURTING

D avid pummeled the punching bag until every ounce of his energy was spent. The gym stank of stale sweat. David's whole face and neck dripped with perspiration. He huffed as he wiped his forehead with the back of his arm.

"Mr. Marks, sorry to disturb you."

David threw his fist into the bag one last time and exhaled.

"What is it, Robert?" He picked up his flask and gulped down the ice water. Robert stood a few feet away and kept a distance between them. David had been in a foul mood since he returned. All of the staff were keeping a wide berth.

"Your father is on the phone—"

"I don't want to speak to him."

"—he's says it's time."

The words sank like heavy rocks in the bottom of his stomach. He pulled his gloves off and sighed. "Right," he said. "Tell him I'm on my way."

The sunshine made everything glow yellow in the garden, and the birds chirped softly in the aviary. There was a gentle breeze in the air and a strange sense of peace. David took a deep breath, as he caught sight of the people standing around the bed. The large glass doors had been rolled back, and as he entered the summer house, he could still hear the tide of the ocean.

Charles stood next to the head of the bed, with his hands resting on the white bony hand of his mother. Edward and Catherine stood at the foot of the bed and watched silently as David stooped down to kiss his grandmother on the forehead.

"Where is your wife, David?" her voice was weak and fragile. Every labored breath seemed to drain her energy.

"She's so sorry she couldn't be here," David lied. He was grateful that Edward didn't retort or make a sound.

"Hold onto that girl. She's got fire in her belly and eyes only for you."

"Grandmother—"

"I know what you're thinking. Don't you worry. I know all about the plan."

David looked up at Charles with surprise and glanced over at Edward who smiled at him. *Why is he smiling?*

"David, my dear, do you think I would be so cruel?"

"I'm sorry? I don't follow—" David was shocked to the core. He'd refused to allow himself to be truly angry with his grandmother and her sudden shift in the will. After all, she was his grandmother. But had she really deceived him?

Grandmother Marks coughed and wheezed.

"It was her plan all along."

He glanced at his co-conspirator father.

"Mission: get David a nice wife," she whispered with a weak smile.

"But how—"

"David," his father started, "you're in your thirties and you still haven't even plucked up the courage to date. Your grandmother—"

"—did not want to die knowing her sweet grandson was doomed to be alone," Grandmother Marks finished for Charles. David looked at everyone in turn. Edward shrugged and laughed; Catherine was smiling at him compassionately. Only Charles looked apologetic.

"You were all in on it?" David asked. Edward raised his hand in defeat.

"You got me. Though I'm insulted you think I would dissolve the family business just to make a new Las Vegas, catering to only rich people." The room laughed quietly at the absurdity of the idea.

"I can't believe the lengths you've all gone to get me married," David said mostly to himself.

"We knew you would only be pushed if there was a worthy cause, and losing the family business and all we've worked so hard to achieve…," Charles explained evenly.

"But I don't understand, when the press came out with that story…."

"What were we supposed to do? We were with guests when the news came on, so we had to keep in character and not let out what we'd done. We still have no idea how that information got out. Our attorneys have sworn they didn't break confidentiality.'"

"But why couldn't you have just explained… Emily won't return my calls. She's—she's—"

"Humiliated? She wonders if any of it was real," Catherine spoke up in her sing-song voice. She placed a hand gently on David's arm. "You need to give her some time. Then go to her, David, and prove to her how you truly feel, and honestly—" She looked over at the family with a slight reprimand before continuing. "—beg her for forgiveness."

"But how?"

"You'll work it out," Grandmother Marks said in a raspy voice. David looked at her with tears in his eyes. She didn't want him to be alone, so she'd orchestrated a whole plan to manipulate him to pursue Emily. He battled equally with being annoyed and touched by the ridiculous ruse.

"Promise me, David," she said, he leaned in close to hear her quiet voice. "Go and get her back. She loves you, and you love her. I always know these things."

David took a deep breath and nodded.

"I promise."

It was a mixture of emotions swirling in his chest. Horrendous grief at saying goodbye to his grandmother, who had just proven that she always had his best interest at heart. And the bubble of hope that he could explain everything to Emily and persuade her to come back to him.

CHAPTER TWENTY-FIVE

THREE MONTHS LATER

E mily missed David. She wanted to hate him, and for three months, she resisted the temptation to call him. She spent most of the time hidden from the public eye, waiting for the media storm to die down, and hadn't even gone into work, but worked from home securing the businesses finances.

The truth was, she was not innocent in this situation. They both had their own agendas. The fact that David's family had set her up was what made her feel so nauseous. And David went along with it. He claimed he didn't know. He left messages for her every day and begged for her forgiveness.

She wanted to. If only she could ignore his family and start over with David, run away to their own island and start a new life. She ached to be with him. Now, so much time had passed, she wasn't sure how. But one thing was certain, she needed to make things right.

Emily stood outside an apartment building in the rain holding a black umbrella and buzzed the number written down on a piece of paper in her hand.

"Who is it?" the voice crackled out of the speaker.

"Emily Stewart," she shouted over the noise of the rain.

Silence.

"I'm not angry with you. In fact, I came here to apologize."

No one answered, but the buzz told Emily she was being granted entry. Emily pulled her umbrella down and shook the rain from it as she walked through the front door. Climbing the steps, she thought about what she was going to say. After a few days of self-pity, consuming far too much ice cream, and watching endless hours of *Friends*, the sadness came in ebbs and flows. She wondered who tipped off the press. Surely, none of David's staff would have sold him out, and the only other person who knew what was really happening was in this building.

She stopped in front of door 111 and knocked. The door opened to reveal a slight woman standing with her arms crossed, and with her a scrawny ginger-haired male, who looked barely eighteen.

He must be the boyfriend.

"I know it was you, Jaqueline," Emily said softly. Jaqueline glanced at the young man next to her and shifted uncomfortably.

"I'm not going to apologize, if that's what you're after." Emily was again surprised at the strength in her "meek" assistant. Jaqueline had more backbone than she'd ever given her credit for.

"No, I want to thank you," Emily replied. Her words sent Jaqueline's eyebrows flying up to the roof.

"Thank me?"

"If you didn't do what you did, I would never have found out about—"

"—about what?"

Emily bit her lip. It was probably best not to divulge any information, not to someone who had a record of selling gossip to the highest bidder.

"You helped me to realize that I owe you an apology. I haven't treated you very well," Emily said carefully. Jaqueline lowered her defensive stance and unfolded her arms. Emily took that as a bid to continue.

"I said you could start taking on clients, then I told you to move to LA with me."

"And you told her to break up with me," the ginger-male retorted, his nostrils flared as he spoke. Emily inclined her head at him.

"I'm sorry for that as well." She turned back to Jaqueline, who lifted a hand up to stop her.

"Not only that, you left Julian in charge. Do you know how awful he is to work with? The sexist comments... the leering. He makes all of us feel uncomfortable in the office. You had to have known."

Emily stared at her open-mouthed for a moment. In all the years she had worked with Julian, he had always been professional with her.

"Honestly, I should have realized, but I just thought Julian was acting like Julian. Why didn't you—"

"—tell you?" Jaqueline added, she scoffed. "You don't listen. Not to anyone. Do you know I'm going to miss my brother's wedding because Julian threatened to fire me if I took the time off? Oh, and he hired me, by the way, but not as the consultant, but as *his* assistant!"

Emily swallowed. How could all of this happen in her company—the business she built up from the very beginning—and she had no idea about any of it?

"I'm so sorry. I will speak to Julian."

Jaqueline closed her mouth and folded her arms again. Apparently lost for words, but still irritated.

"I'm going to make this right, I promise."

"And what about LA?"

Emily shook her head. "No more LA. Looks like New York needs me more," she said heavily. Jaqueline stared at her, apparently searching for any sign of a joke.

"Do you want to come in?" Jaqueline asked tentatively. Emily shook her head.

"No, I have some loose ends to tie up. But I hope you will accept these as a token of my appreciation for all you do." She held out a brown paper bag. Jaqueline peered inside the bag and grinned at her.

"You seem to wear them a lot, and I wanted to find a way to show you I'm being sincere, when I say I'm sorry." She took a nervous breath and studied Jaqueline's look of surprise. "I've been invited to Estelle Magazine's annual charity event, and to prove I mean what I say. I'll be wearing my own pair underneath my gown."

Emily pulled out a pair of pink Crocs from her purse. Jaqueline stifled a laugh and her cheeks flushed with color.

"Go to your brother's wedding." Emily smiled at her. "Let me deal with Julian."

Emily walked into her office and stared blankly as her brain tried to register what she was seeing. A tall, muscular man dressed in a grey suit sat at Emily's desk. The sun reflected off his bald head and he flashed his white teeth as he rested a hand on the knee of his young assistant.

"Get out," Emily said curtly. The young woman jumped up and ran out of the room. The man folded his arms and sat back in the chair until it squeaked under his weight.

"I wasn't expecting you in today," he said smoothly.

Emily dropped her bag on the white couch and rested her hands on his hips.

"Julian, I came to discuss some serious accusations with you. But coming in to see you leering over that young girl is enough for me. You're fired."

Julian's smile faded and he got to his feet.

"Now hold on," he said in a warning tone. "You can't just fire me."

"Well, I can speak to the women in this office and allow them to file a sexual assault claim. We could go to the police and then court, and then I could fire you. Would you prefer that?"

Julian looked at Emily with narrow eyes.

"What's gotten into you today?"

Emily marched over to the window and looked out at New York. She gazed at the hustle and bustle of the people and traffic below. She smiled at the near-constant shrill of horns, despite the "no honking" signs littered along the streets.

"Some common sense has gotten into me," she replied as she turned back to him.

"What about your dream?"

"That's the beauty of dreams, Julian. You can wake up and realize they were not what you wanted." Emily leaned over the desk and placed her hands on the papers.

"All these years we've worked together, and I never realized how much of a creep you are."

"Come on, you didn't even see anything. Nothing happened."

"Really? Is that what Lana is going to say when I ask how you treat her? Is it true you told Jaqueline she couldn't take the day off to go to her brother's wedding?"

Julian's lips were thin as his jaw hardened.

"Give me a month to find another job."

"Fine, but you're not working here. Take it as sick leave."

Julian glared at her as they stood across from each other in a silent stand-off.

"You know it's more than fair," Emily added, her

brow raised. Julian lifted his head and looked down at her with a hint of amusement.

"Fair enough." Without a moment's hesitation, he marched out of the room and closed the door behind her. Emily slumped her shoulders and collapsed into the chair with relief. She felt like she had been holding her breath the entire exchange.

S tanding with her coat raised over her head, trying to shield her gown from getting drenched in the pouring rain, Emily fumbled with her phone to call a cab. This was the biggest event of the year, an opportunity to really get her reputation out there. She might even get to meet Estelle herself. Rumors had it that there would be a red carpet, and all of the important celebrities would be there. She imagined the clients who would be jumping on board once they saw her on TV. It was a perfect networking event to pick up her mood and focus her nervous energy on something productive. She finally found the occasion to wear her Vivienne Westwood gown. It hugged her curves and draped around her body so beautifully, she looked like a human candle-stick. She curled her hair and let it hang loose in waves. As promised, underneath the designer dress, she wore pink crocs. To her surprise, she found them to be the most comfortable shoes she had ever worn. She decided she would always keep a pair under her desk at work.

She got into the cab and looked out of the window as the taxi driver pulled away. She wondered what David was doing. He was never far from her mind, though she often tried to push him back into the corner of her brain. The image of his face stung her heart. She wished there was a way the two of them could have worked things out. Technically they were still married, so she'd have to pick up the phone eventually. She couldn't believe what a fool she had been. How she could fall for someone so quickly, and how had she naively thought they could make it work, when their whole relationship was built on a foundation of lies.

The cab pulled up at a side street near Central Park. Emily paid the driver and slinked out of the cab with ease. The rain had stopped, and the damp sidewalks sparkled under the streetlamps. Pop music flooded the air and the beat of the bass guitar thumped in Emily's ears as she followed the noise. She pushed her shoulders back and swayed her hips as she walked confidently across the street and entered Central Park.

Then she saw it. The cameras flashed endlessly, and a constant stream of black limousines pulled up, celebrities exiting the cars, waving to the crowd, then walking down the red carpet rolled out onto the grass.

"Emily Stewart, Find My Companion," Emily said to the bodyguard at the beginning of the red carpet. He checked his tablet and gave a nod. A small woman handed Emily a lanyard with a VIP badge on it.

"Follow the carpet to the main stage, and you'll be shown to your seat," she said in a heavy New York accent. Emily nodded and stepped out onto the carpet.

"Look!" Cries from the crowd alerted Emily. She wondered if a superstar had just arrived. Cameras flashed even faster, and Emily stood in awe of the blinding flashes. Once her eyes adjusted to the lights, she noticed the cameras were not facing the red carpet, but to the sky instead.

"What on earth?" she whispered under her breath. A hot air balloon hovered in the sky; the blast of the gas was so loud she had to cover her ears. The crowd of people stepped back to give the balloon more space as it slowly lowered and came to a stop with a bump, onto the grass.

"Who is it? Who is it?" The reporters jabbed each other and wrestled to get a good look at who was inside. A tall figure approached the edge of the basket and as the gas fired again, Emily saw him.

David Marks.

"Emily," he called out as he hopped over the edge

of the basket and hurried to her. The crowd was going crazy. Emily could hardly hear his voice. She looked wildly around her at the commotion he'd caused, then her eyes landed back on David's bright eyes.

"I know you find it hard to trust me, or believe anything I say. Because I lied to you," he shouted. "The truth is, we were both lied to, and we lied to each other. But I'm done with lies. I want to tell you everything." Emily looked sheepishly around as David held out his hands to her.

"I had an imaginary friend named Twix until I was twelve. He was a deer." Emily resisted the smile threatening to take over her face. "I had to have hypnosis to help me sleep again after Edward forced me to watch a horror movie about a clown." The crowd chuckled and the reporters were still taking photos. Emily wondered how many photos they could possibly need. "I used to tell people that I designed the Eiffel Tower."

Emily snorted. "Who would believe that?"

"My grandmother died. But not before she told me the truth."

"And what is that?" Emily shouted back, trying to be heard over the roar of the crowd and the incessant flash of cameras. He lowered down on bended knee.

"That you can't fake love. It happens whether you like it or not. And I can't go on another moment

239

without asking you, truthfully. Emily Stewart, will you be my wife?"

The crowd erupted into cheers and the reporters were going wild. Fighting to get the best picture and people were chanting in the background.

They were already married. Emily looked up at the starry sky and her gaze hovered over the balloon. She realized it had huge sunflowers on it. Emily looked down at David to see him holding a small box with his grandmother's ring. His gaze burned into her. She was overwhelmed. The music thumped against her temples, and the screeching crowds sent her senses into a frenzy. She wasn't sure if it was David's speech, or the overwhelming chaos around them, but she lowered all her defences and nodded her head.

"All right, for real, this time?" She beamed. David pushed the ring onto her finger and lifted her up into his arms.

"Just promise me one thing," Emily said as she hovered near his lips.

"Anything."

"That we will never lie to each other again."

David grinned and nodded like an excitable puppy. He swooped her around in a circle and they kissed. She closed her eyes and thought that somewhere there were fireworks going off, cheers and screams filled the air.

Emily and David broke apart and laughed at the crowd as they waved to the reporters, hand in hand.

"Do you want to find a seat?" David asked.

Emily's head was spinning. Suddenly, the idea of schmoozing with a load of celebrities didn't seem so appealing. Emily pointed at the hot air balloon.

"You know, I've never been in one of those before," she said. David tightened his grip on her and appeared to follow her line of thought. Then he walked her to the balloon and lifted her over the edge of the basket. The Vivienne Westwood gown draped away from her feet and she was certain the reporters got several shots of the bright pink crocs. She didn't care.

David jumped inside the basket and turned to her.

"I love you Emily." He cradled her face with his hands.

Emily pulled him in and kissed David and moaned into his mouth. He held the small of her back and they explored each other, blissfully unaware of their surroundings. They broke apart panting and Emily rested her hand over his heart; she could feel it beating against her palm. She was still furious with Charles. There was a lot to talk about, and so much she still didn't know about David. But she had no doubt about one thing; she was happier when he was around. He made the world feel right again, and even with hidden agendas and manipulating family members in the mix, being with David felt right. At the end of it all, what did it matter how they met? *It will make a great story*, she figured as she stroked a tuft of his wavy hair and gazed lovingly into his eyes. And with that thought she simply said, "I love you more."

T he End

27186293R00147

Printed in Great Britain
by Amazon